MARKET BOO[...]
IF RETURNED
WE WILL ALLOW
OTHER BOOKS.

CW00709144

A low growl sounded in Lee's throat and he gathered her possessively closer, thrusting his body hard against hers.

The logical, thinking part of Jo's brain was hazily aware of what was happening. . .warning her it was madness to let this go on. Perversely, her heart resisted. Her lips burned with hungry need and she wanted him to go on kissing the fire away. Against all rational thought, her body wanted his exploring, arousing hands against her tingling skin.

She'd daydreamed over his photographs. . .perhaps even fantasised a little. . .wondered. . .it had seemed harmless enough.

But the Lee who held her so fiercely, his mind bent on some kind of savage retribution, wasn't the man she'd daydreamed over. He was what he had always been: a complete stranger.

MARKET BOOKSTALL-LANCA
IF RETURNED IN GOOD CONDITIC
WE WILL ALLOW HALF PRICE TOWARDS
OTHER BOOKS

MISTAKEN LOVE

BY

SHIRLEY KEMP

MILLS & BOON LIMITED
ETON HOUSE   18–24 PARADISE ROAD
RICHMOND   SURREY   TW9 1SR

All the characters in this book have no existence outside the imagination of the Author, and have no relation whatsoever to anyone bearing the same name or names. They are not even distantly inspired by any individual known or unknown to the Author, and all the incidents are pure invention.

All Rights Reserved. The text of this publication or any part thereof may not be reproduced or transmitted in any form or by any means, electronic or mechanical, including photocopying, recording, storage in an information retrieval system, or otherwise, without the written permission of the publisher.

This book is sold subject to the condition that it shall not, by way of trade or otherwise, be lent, resold, hired out or otherwise circulated without the prior consent of the publisher in any form of binding or cover other than that in which it is published and without a similar condition including this condition being imposed on the subsequent purchaser.

First published in Great Britain 1991
by Mills & Boon Limited

© Shirley Kemp 1991

Australian copyright 1991
Philippine copyright 1991
This edition 1991

ISBN 0 263 77094 X

Set in 10½ on 12 pt Linotron Times
01-9105-46911
Typeset in Great Britain by Centracet, Cambridge
Made and printed in Great Britain

CHAPTER ONE

AT LONG last, the plane touched down. Stiff and aching, Joanne clambered slowly down the steps.

She managed, almost in a daze, to get through the Customs and out of the airport building, on to the wide, clean pavement. She stood blinking in the unfamiliar sunshine, feeling lost and rather shaky.

'Would you like a cab, lady?'

A dour-faced man, with a toothpick in the corner of his mouth, and the peak of his cap turned to the back of his head, stood beside a shiny saloon car.

'Yes, please.' Joanne let out a sigh of relief.

The driver grasped her case and strode away, leaving her to follow, almost at a trot in her unaccustomed high heels, wincing as they pinched her feet. She'd worn them to mark the occasion, but had already begun to wish that common sense had taken the place of pride.

The driver opened his rear door and, with an imperious hand, gestured her to get inside. She sank gratefully into the deep, cool upholstery.

'Where to, lady?'

Joanne fumbled in her handbag for the address, made more clumsy by the impatient tapping of the driver's sinewy hand against the steering-wheel. At last, she found the crumpled piece of paper and handed it to him through the glass partition. Without a word, he nodded and handed it back.

As the car moved smoothly off, she settled back and spread the sheet of paper, smoothing it against her knee. It was a letter, dated more than two months earlier. The last in a succession of letters from her twin Jocelyn, full of excitement and vivid descriptions of Lee Staddon, her American fiancé and her new life with him in Florida.

For the past six months, the letters had come almost weekly, along with photographs of herself and Lee and of every conceivable part of the beautiful house that would be her home when they were married.

Jo read the letter through once more and frowned, wondering, as she had wondered many times in the past two months, why they had suddenly stopped.

She and Jocelyn had never been as close as identical twins were reputed to be, but her sister's obvious happiness had somehow drawn them closer together. Jo had been relieved to think that her highly strung and rather unpredictable twin had at last found happiness with a man who appeared perfect in every way.

Jo delved once more into her handbag for the photograph of a dark, smiling man. She ran her fingers over its glossy surface, thinking how strange it was that she knew every inch of Lee Staddon's face, from the calm, dark, laughing eyes to the slightly curving strength of his nose and the warm sensuality of his slightly full lips. She knew well, in her imagination, the springy texture of his thick hair, framing the strong, manly face. And yet he was a stranger.

Gazing at the photograph now, she felt the odd, unsettling sensation which always seemed to affect her whenever she looked at it. Soon, she would actually see him in the flesh, she thought with a tingle of anticipation. And what had seemed like bad luck at the time had, in fact, been the means by which her surprise visit had suddenly become possible.

If the company she'd been working for since she'd left secretarial school hadn't gone bust, making her redundant, it was doubtful she ever would have seen him, since it was unlikely she could ever have afforded the money to make the visit, not even for the wedding. As it was, the trip would take a large bite out of the small amount of compensation she'd been paid. But it would all be worth it. . .to see Jocelyn settled and happy with the man she obviously loved very much. And in such lovely surroundings too! Lucky Jocelyn, she thought with a twinge of envy as she remembered the grey skies she'd left behind and which she would be seeing again all too soon.

She sighed. She didn't want to think about it now, but when she got back in two weeks' time she would have to start looking for another job to keep the wolf from the door. Never mind, she told herself doggedly. This was going to be the holiday of a lifetime and she was determined to enjoy every minute. She could worry about her finances any old time and she wasn't going to let anxiety about the future spoil her pleasure now.

On the journey over, she'd been calm in a detached sort of way, almost as though it were some other self engaged on this impulsive adventure. But now her nerves were tingling with a mixture of apprehension and anticipation.

Doubts crowded into her mind. Perhaps she should have telephoned to let them know she was coming; but, naïvely, she'd wanted to surprise Jocelyn. Now she had time to worry whether her surprise would be more of an embarrassment than a pleasure. She should have written for Lee's permission.

Jo let out her breath. Oh, well! She had almost arrived. It was too late to worry about it now.

She folded the letter and put it back into its envelope, with the photograph carefully tucked inside. Determinedly, she directed her attention to the unfamiliar surroundings passing swiftly by. They had already left the busy thoroughfares of the city. Across wide, neatly trimmed lawns and between tall leafy trees, Jo caught enticing glimpses of splendid residences, too grand to be called houses.

It was a bright day and the sun slanted through the window, warming her shoulder. She revelled in the sheer luxury of it all.

After a while, exhausted by the long flight and lulled by the smooth purring movement of the car, she fell into a light doze. She woke when the taxi drew to a halt.

Jo blinked her eyes open and stared at the large

house before which they'd halted. Gleaming white in the sun, its gardens ablaze with brilliant flowers. . .it was even lovelier than the photographs had led her to expect.

'This is it.'

The driver got out and hauled her case on to the drive at the bottom of a flight of wide stone steps.

'OK, lady?' He pushed the toothpick to the other side of his mouth and scratched his head beneath his cap. Almost as an afterthought, he opened the rear door for her to get out.

'Thanks.' Jo stood rather shakily in the driveway. 'How much do I owe you?'

The man named an extortionate amount and Jo felt herself blanch. She'd changed what she had thought was a reasonable sum into dollars, but it went nowhere near to covering the fare. Obviously, life here was going to be very much more expensive than she had anticipated. Now what? she asked herself fretfully.

'I ain't got all day, ya know,' the driver broke into her anxious thoughts.

Jo felt a flash of irritation. For the kind of money he was demanding, he could afford to be a little more polite.

'I'm afraid you'll have to wait a little longer,' she said with asperity, but she felt nothing like as brave as she sounded as she walked up the steps to the house. For long seconds, she stood before the imposing front door, trying to pluck up the courage to ring the bell. It was one thing to pay an unexpected visit, but quite another to come begging for a loan before

she'd even had time to introduce herself to her
future brother-in-law.

She squared her shoulders and lifted her hand to
the bell, but, before she had time to touch it, the
door was flung open by a large woman who stared at
her in disbelief.

'Why, Miss Jocelyn!' she gasped. 'I saw the cab
coming, but I wasn't expecting to see you back here.'

The woman thought she was Jocelyn! Jo returned
her stare, her mind suddenly blank. Her mouth
opened, but no sound came out.

'You gonna pay me, lady, or what?' The driver
was becoming aggressive.

The big woman clucked disapprovingly. 'You
bring that bag up here, man, if you wanna be paid.'

'I'm afraid. . .' Jo suddenly found her voice. 'I
haven't quite enough to pay the fare.'

'Don't worry. Emie will get it from the
housekeeping.'

Emie! The name popped suddenly into Jo's
memory. Jocelyn had sent her a photograph of Lee's
housekeeper in her large, shiny kitchen.

She bustled past, carrying Jo's case.

'You come right in.' And, as Jo hesitated, she cast
a look over her shoulder that was full of understanding. 'I don't blame you for being scared. Mr Lee's
been real mad since you went.'

Jo's brain was reeling as she followed Emie's large
rear into a bright, airy hallway, thickly carpeted and
furnished with gleaming oak.

The housekeeper halted and put down Jo's case.

'Um,' Jo began hesitantly, 'I'm afraid you don't understand. . . I'm not. . .'

As Emie's enquiring brown eyes turned on Jo, a door at the far end of the hallway opened and a man came out.

Joanne's heart lurched as she recognised him. Tall, dark and compellingly handsome, Lee Staddon stood there, staring at Jo as though he'd seen a ghost.

'Hell!' he cried explosively, his voice seeming to rasp in his throat. 'I don't believe this!' His dark eyes riveted coldly on her face as he came towards her. 'You've got a nerve—coming back here. . .'

Mesmerised by the speed of his approach and the anger blazing in his eyes, Jo stared back speechless.

With a sudden movment, he grasped her arms. 'Why did you come back?'

Jo flinched from his rough hands. . .the hard face he thrust into hers.

'Let go of me,' she cried angrily. 'You don't understand——'

His harsh laugh cut across. 'And you're going to help me with that? Am I right?' A cynical gleam shone in his eyes. 'Well, I guess I'm curious enough to listen to your explanations.'

He released her suddenly, thrusting her away from him so forcefully that she staggered.

'But I can't guarantee to believe what I hear.'

'Please,' Jo cried fiercely, regaining her balance and rubbing at her arms, which burned painfully. 'Listen to me——'

'Not now.' Lee waved a dismissive hand, refusing

to let her finish. 'Save it for later. I'll be here for
dinner. Right now, I'm going out.'

The front door slammed behind him and Jo was
left alone with Emie, confused and visibly shaken.

'I guess you're tired.' Emie's shrewd brown eyes
looked compassionately into Jo's pale face. 'Maybe
you'll feel better after dinner.' She squeezed Jo's
arm comfortingly. 'I'll get Sidonie to take your bag
up.'

She pressed a bell set in the panelling. It echoed
somewhere in the back of the house and almost
immediately a young girl came out of a doorway
beneath the staircase.

'Take Miss Jocelyn's bags up right away and run
her a bath.'

Sidonie nodded and lifted Jo's case.

'Your maid's gone,' Emie told Jo. 'Mr Lee didn't
see no point in keeping her on after you went. You'll
have to make do with my kitchen help till you two
get yourselves sorted out.'

She wiped her hands together, as though divorcing
herself from any trouble that might be brewing.

'Now I got to go and get on with dinner.'

Jo's head was swimming. Everything had moved
so fast, she had trouble thinking straight. 'Emie,
I——'

But the housekeeper was gone.

Turning to Sidonie, Jo began again. 'I'm
afraid. . .'

But it was the wrong time. . .the wrong person. . .

Jo's shoulders rose and fell in a defeated shrug.
'Never mind. Lead on. I'll follow you up.'

Later, she promised herself as she followed Sidonie up the wide staircase. Later. . .when she'd had a chance to tidy herself up and rest a little, she would seek Lee out and explain. And, hopefully, he would repay the courtesy and explain what this was all about.

But at the moment she was suddenly yearning for nothing more than a long soak in a nice warm bath.

The house was even more luxurious than the photographs had led Jo to expect. Sidonie led her across a gallery which overhung the hall and then into a wide corridor, where she opened a door into a large bedroom. She put Jo's case down and crossed to another door at the far end.

'I'll just run your bath.'

Jo heard the sound of running water and sat down tiredly on the end of the large bed, while her eyes wandered about the room.

'You sure do look whacked, miss.' The maid was back in the room. 'But don't worry! There's plenty of time for you to rest before dinner. If you like, I'll give you a call when it's near ready.'

The girl's eyes were fixed on Jo's face, full of concern. But behind that Jo saw the gleam of curiosity.

'Thank you.'

When the girl had gone, Jo inspected the bedroom. The whole of one wall was a huge wardrobe and she slid back the mirrored doors to reveal racks and racks of beautiful clothes, slim, elegant clothes. . .so obviously the type Jocelyn loved to wear. In this collection, Jocelyn would look absolutely stunning. How and why had she gone, leaving them all behind?

Lee's face flashed suddenly into her mind—not as she had seen it in the photographs, but as she had seen it in the hall. . .hard and angry, with a cynical curving smile that seemed to promise he could be cruel as well as sensual, and revealing a side Jocelyn hadn't even hinted at in her letters. They had been full of how wonderful he was. . .how kind he was. . .how much he adored her. But where was Jocelyn now? And what had gone wrong?

With a sigh, she sank back on to the bed, unanswerable questions whirling in her brain. She closed her eyes, fatigue washing over her, making her drowsy.

When she woke later, the bath water was cold and she had to take a hurried shower before rummaging in her case for something suitable to wear.

Sidonie came as she was trying to make up her mind between her one and only evening dress and a cool cotton day dress. Did Lee expect her to dress formally?

The sun still shone through the tall windows, which overlooked a rear garden the size of a park. It seemed suddenly impossible to believe she was actually here and about to go down to dinner with the man she had thought about and speculated over for so long.

But now, she felt no pleasure. The thought of facing Lee again had her knees shaking. Devoid of the wide smile that had captivated her in his photographs, his face had seemed hewn out of granite. There could be no doubt he was a hard man to cross, and whatever Jocelyn had done to earn his displeasure it was Jo who would now feel the brunt of it.

Mentally, she steeled herself. If she kept calm and explained quietly, it was bound to defuse the situation. She must just try to stay cool.

In the end, she chose the evening dress to give herself a little moral support. It was straight, simple and unsophisticated, but the delicate shade of green brought out the russet lights in her chestnut hair and softened the blue of her eyes. The clean lines clung closely to her figure. As she walked down the curving staircase, excitement warred with mounting apprehension.

CHAPTER TWO

LEE STADDON'S reaction to Jo's appearance was startling.

He was standing in the doorway of the elegant dining-room when she reached the bottom of the staircase. For a second, his eyes opened wide in what seemed obvious appreciation and Jo thought she glimpsed a longing in them before the thick lashes swept it away.

'Your little vacation must have done you good,' he said abruptly. 'You look positively stunning.'

Jocelyn would probably have taken the compliment for granted, but Jo, unused to praise, flushed deeply. 'Thank you.'

He led her into the room and held a chair for her with cold courtesy. She sat at the highly polished table, waiting in silence for him to sit down, but he remained standing and she looked up at him uncertainly.

'I'm flattered you've taken the trouble to dress for dinner,' he said with heavy irony, 'but, unfortunately, I have to go out. We'll have to postpone our little tête-à-tête for another time.'

There was a taunting expression on his face that told her he was enjoying some kind of cat-and-mouse game. Despite the cool smile, she sensed his antagonism, the latent fury seething beneath the calm façade. He still thought she was Jocelyn, and was taking an obvious delight in keeping her twin dangling.

She took a deep breath. 'Lee,' she began with desperate determination. 'I have to talk to you.'

'It'll keep,' he responded shortly.

Jo shook her head in exasperation. 'You don't understand. You're making a mistake——'

'Past tense, my dear,' he broke in with a short laugh. 'I *made* a mistake. It's one I won't be repeating.'

For a moment, Jo thought she saw the hurt which lurked beneath the bitterness, and put an impulsive hand on his sleeve.

'Lee,' she said softly, 'I wish you'd let me explain.'

He shook her off. 'As I said. . .it'll keep.'

He moved away abruptly, as though he couldn't stand to be near her, and, embarrassed, Jo wished she hadn't given way to impulse.

'Unfortunately, my date won't. So, if you'll excuse me.'

He left without another word, and, despite her frustration, Jo found herself wondering if the date that wouldn't keep was a woman.

She ate dinner alone in the elegant dining-room. When it was over, she felt suddenly dog-tired.

Her holiday could hardly have begun on a more uncomfortable note, she thought, as she went disconsolately up to bed. Tomorrow, she would *make* Lee listen to her. But, even if she managed to do that, it wouldn't make things any easier. Jocelyn, her infuriating and unpredictable twin, had left Lee, and there was no way he could be expected to welcome her sister on a surprise visit.

She kept seeing his eyes as they widened in appreciation and the thought gave her a funny feeling in the pit of her stomach. He'd thought he was looking at Jocelyn, she reminded herself hastily, but he'd still admired her. . .called her stunning!

Although she felt worn out, she couldn't sleep. The luxurious strangeness of her surroundings and the mystery of Jocelyn's broken romance kept her tense and uneasy. Even in the comfort of the big bed, she tossed and turned restlessly.

How could things have possibly gone so wrong between Lee and Jocelyn? Jo could have sworn that, this time, Jocelyn had been in love. Her letters had been so happy. . .so full of Lee. Why had she gone off, leaving him behind? Lee. . .who seemed everything she'd ever dreamt of and talked about since she was a girl. It didn't make sense.

No more questions, she told herself tiredly. There was only one person who could answer them at the moment, and he wasn't even prepared to listen to her. This whole silly misunderstanding would never have arisen, she told herself fretfully, if he had only been prepared to spare her a little of his time and attention.

Well, tomorrow she would insist on having both; but the resolution did little to calm her nerves. An hour later, she was still wide awake. . .still puzzling. . .and still restless.

With a sigh of exasperation, she got out of bed and padded about the room, looking for something to read, anything to distract her mind from its circular thinking, but there wasn't a book or magazine anywhere to be found. Not really surprising, she reminded herself ruefully, since Jocelyn had never been one to sit quietly and read. The fact that her letters had been so long and descriptive had surprised Jo and it was that, as much as anything else, that had persuaded her that this time her sister really had changed.

But there must be something to read somewhere in the house, she told herself irritably. She chewed her lip, wondering if she could find her way to the study. With all the information Jocelyn had given her, it shouldn't be too difficult to find. She crossed the room and went out into the corridor, where dim lights burned.

Treading softly, she made her way down the broad staircase. In her head, she held a mental plan of the house, but once in the hall she hesitated, trying to work out which door led to the study. She chose the one to the rear of the hall, the one she had seen Lee come out of when she'd arrived.

She opened the door and, in the dim light from the hallway, found the light switch. She snapped it on and stepped inside. The bright light illuminated the gleaming floor, the orderly shelves of books lining the walls.

She'd found it! She smiled and allowed herself a small mental pat on the back. The next moment the smile was wiped away by a gasp of shock, as her eyes fixed on the dark head of the man who had been sleeping on a day-bed in one corner. He raised himself on to one elbow to stare at her.

'I'm. . .sorry.' Jo flushed to the roots of her hair. What on earth was he doing sleeping in the study? she wondered as she struggled with her embarrassment. 'I. . . I was looking for something to read.'

'Something to read,' he repeated laconically, and Jo began to feel uneasy.

He swung his legs easily out of bed and Joanne gaped at his unselfconscious nakedness. Unable to help herself, she stared open-mouthed at his tanned and firmly muscled body.

'See anything you haven't seen before?' he drawled.

Jo snapped her mouth shut and took a deep breath, trying to regain her poise. Of course, there was no way he could know it was the first time she had seen any man naked, but if she could help it he wasn't going to guess that.

She had been unprepared for the beauty of him. It took a conscious effort to tear her eyes away.

'There's something I've been trying to tell you,' she muttered uncomfortably. 'Do you think we could talk now?'

'Oh, sure!' The hard cynicism in his voice made her look at him again. She was relieved to see he had put on a towelling robe.

'We could start with Burt Keegan,' he said, with suddenly menacing softness. 'The guy you ran away with. What happened? Did you get fed up and dump him too?' He came close, staring into her wide and suddenly wary eyes. 'Or did he dump you?' He grasped her shoulders roughly. 'Is that why you've come back to me?'

'Burt Keegan?' Jo repeated uncomprehendingly. 'I'm afraid I——'

'Can't quite recall the name,' Lee finished, with heavy sarcasm. He gave a short, unpleasant laugh. 'Have you forgotten his existence already—as quickly as you forgot mine?'

Jo shook her head in denial, but suddenly things were beginning to make sense. There was another man involved. . .something she hadn't anticipated, and yet typical of Jocelyn.

'You don't understand,' she said weakly.

'Oh, I think I do.' He drew her closer, his fingers biting into the soft flesh of her upper arms. 'Were you hoping I'd say all is forgiven and fall into your arms, as I did the first time we met?' He nodded, with a slow, cynical smile. 'Yes. A passionate reconciliation would be just your style.'

Without warning, his lips were on hers, his arms slipping about her to draw her fiercely against him, his hard chest crushing her breast. Her heart thudded wildly and she felt his heartbeat like a crazy echo of her own. She struggled against the bruising pressure of his lips, the iron strength of his hold, twisting her body, frantically trying to free herself. But her efforts seemed only to inflame him. . .to increase his determined strength, as her own ebbed. A small, helpless cry sounded in her throat.

His head lifted at the sound, and he stared down at her, his eyes coldly triumphant.

'Aren't you enjoying this?' he asked mockingly.

'If you came hoping to prove the power of that lovely body, then you have it. . .here.' He clasped Jo's hand and guided it beneath his robe to the hard proof of his arousal. 'That should tell you something.' His mouth twisted in a grimace of a smile. 'It seems you can still make me want you.'

Jo gave a cry and snatched her hand away, shocked by the sensations the contact aroused. Her insides were churning dizzily. . .her mouth was suddenly dry.

He gave a low laugh, which sounded dangerously ragged.

Desperately, she pushed against his chest, creating a little space, and gasped air into her aching lungs. 'Lee—please stop,' she pleaded unevenly. 'You don't have to do this.'

'Oh, but I do.'

Again his lips claimed hers, but this time softly, slowly, in a deep, exploring kiss that took her unawares and sent fiery sparks of delight shooting through her. The shock of what he had just revealed seemed to have aroused unknown feelings. As his hand stroked the length of her painfully sensitised spine, Jo found, to her horror, that she was shaking. Even as she struggled for control, a spontaneous kind of excitement flared inside her and suddenly she was responding, her body arching towards him, her mouth moving hungrily against his in a searching exploration of its own.

A low growl sounded in Lee's throat and he gathered her possessively closer, thrusting his body hard against hers as she clung to him.

The logical, thinking part of Jo's brain was hazily aware of what was happening. . .warning her it was madness to let this go on. Perversely, her heart resisted. Her lips burned with hungry need and she wanted him to go on kissing the fire away. Against all rational thought, her body wanted his exploring, arousing hands against her tingling skin.

Desperately, she tried to reason against the sudden, unbidden needs of her own body.

She'd daydreamed over his photographs. . .perhaps even fantasised a little. . .wondered. . .it had seemed harmless enough. But the Lee who held her so fiercely, his mind bent on some kind of savage retribution, wasn't the man she'd daydreamed over. He was what he had always been: a complete stranger.

Some last vestige of common sense made her resist as he drew her towards the bed. . .slid the lacy nightgown from her shoulders.

This isn't real, she told herself desperately. He wants the woman he thinks you are. . . Jocelyn. It was Jocelyn he thought he was kissing. His passion, punishingly sweet, was meant for her. Whatever Jocelyn had done, Jo reminded herself, she was still Lee's fiancée. She was still the woman he wanted now.

As she wrenched her mouth from his, he looked at her, his eyes dark and lucent, probing her own.

She stared back, her eyes wide, still glistening with awakened passion, her breath audibly ragged in her throat.

'Lee—don't,' she whispered then, her voice ending on an uneven sigh. 'Please.'

He touched her cheek, gently exploring, his eyes suddenly narrowed, a tiny frown between his brows. His lips moved as though a question hung there, but he said nothing. Slowly, his hand lifted to smooth the hair from her face, to lift its heavy weight away from her neck. His lips descended to the warm column of her throat, moving tenderly, washing away her will.

Heated spears of sensation pierced her body and her arms slid around his neck as she clung to him. She heard the sharp intake of his breath, felt the tightening of his hold, the tension in his body.

His lips caressed her throat, swept across the smooth softness of her shoulders, trailing kisses down to the swell of her breast as the lace fell away under his fingers. Undreamt of sensations filled her and a moan sighed softly past her lips.

He looked up then and a smile lifted the corners of his lips. His hands caressed her breasts, making her want to clutch at him, pull his head down to her. He moved the nightdress lower and she shivered with anticipation. Her conscience tried desperately to resurrect her from the heady mists of desire. Seconds more and she would be lost.

Then his hand, which had been moving maddeningly against the full under-curve of her breast, stilled. Slowly, he drew away, a wondering expression on his face.

Jo's eyes flew questioningly to his. Her heart beat so loudly, she was sure he could hear it. . .see its wild beating in the base of her throat. She swallowed and waited.

He looked back at her for long seconds, searching her face intently. Then, slowly, he released her.

'I—I'm. . .sorry,' he said at last, a frown between his dark brows. 'I. . .that. . .was a—mistake. Forgive me.'

Jo sat up, dazed and bewildered, her emotions a mixture of reluctance and relief, a confusion of gratitude for her last-minute salvation and humiliation at her near surrender.

If he hadn't moved away. . .could she have done?

Lee turned from her. Calmly, he leaned towards a shelf above the divan and took down a book. His eyes were cool and unreadable as he handed it to her.

'You were looking for a book, I believe,' he said. 'Let me know what you think of that one.'

CHAPTER THREE

JOANNE sat on the bed, picking disconsolately at the cold remains of breakfast. She still felt confused and vaguely depressed by the happenings of the past hours. That was all it was, a matter of hours, since she had stepped inside this house and become enmeshed in a tangled web which, despite her best efforts, she had been unable to unravel.

Somehow it seemed much longer than that, and the purpose of her visit had become obscured by the unexpected situation and Lee's hostile attitude.

All through the night, her mind had been full of Lee, her dreams a rerun of the disturbing moments she'd spent in his arms. All the more disturbing, because she knew she would have let him make love to her. She had wanted him, despite her inner warnings that she was betraying her sister and her own conscience.

Even now, she felt the humiliation. Why had she let herself respond to him so eagerly? He had used his lovemaking perversely, roughly at first and then disguised as tenderness. And, almost unconsciously, she had responded to that tenderness. Somehow, against all common sense, she'd been caught up in his mistaken love.

He was convinced she was Jocelyn. Had his certainty undermined her own sense of identity? No, she told herself firmly, she couldn't hide behind that as an excuse. Growing up, she'd always been aware of the differences between them and, despite their mother's apparent preference for Jocelyn, had never been envious of her twin.

Why not settle for heat of the moment and the power of chemical attraction? she told herself facetiously in an attempt to bring some perspective to the situation. She hadn't let him make love to her, so no harm had been done. Her mind skirted quickly around the fact that it had been he, and not she, who had finally drawn away.

There was no point in dwelling on what had happened. . .in trying to unravel the tangled skein of emotions he aroused. The best she could do was vow that it wouldn't happen again. From now on, she would be on her guard, against herself as much as against him.

With a gesture of impatience, she pushed the breakfast trolley away. What did it matter anyway, since she wouldn't be here much longer?

Once Lee found out who she was, she could hardly expect him to welcome her as a guest in his house. It was obvious, after last night, that he still wanted Jocelyn physically, but there had been no forgiveness in him. The seeds of bitterness were still deep within him.

She paced the room, her bottom lip held abstractedly between her teeth. If it had been difficult before to reveal her identity, it was going to be doubly difficult now, after what had taken place between them. Her stomach did a double somersault at the thought of facing him. She would need all the poise and dignity she could muster to get through the ordeal.

Oh, well, she shrugged mentally, it had to be done—and sooner rather than later.

She bathed quickly and dressed in the first thing that came to hand: a cool yellow cotton dress, which matched the sunshine of the morning, but made a stark contrast to the turmoil within her. Her face, with only a trace of make-up, looked pale and uncertain. She hoped her vulnerability wouldn't be too obvious to Lee.

With a final dissatisfied look at her reflection, she went out of the room and down the stairs.

She could hear Emie's strong tones carrying clearly from the kitchen and Sidonie's high young voice replying. They were obviously busy with the preparations for lunch.

Straightening her shoulders, Jo pushed determinedly at the kitchen door. 'Is Lee about?'

Two heads turned in her direction; two pairs of eyes regarding her curiously.

'Why, no.' Emie wiped her large hands on a paper towel before turning around to give Jo her full attention. 'He's gone to the office like always. He said to tell you he'd be home around lunch. . .if you was to ask.'

'Oh!'

Joanne's heart sank. Having hyped herself up to the task of facing Lee, it was galling to find that, once again, he had eluded her.

'Well. . . I. . . I suppose I'll just have to wait until then.'

Emie's grin was sly. 'Honey! I wish you luck.'

'I think I'm going to need it,' Jo muttered to herself as she made her escape.

Out in the hall, she was suddenly at a loss. To go back to the bedroom and think about what lay ahead would drive her mad.

Longing for distraction from her painful thoughts, she crossed the hall into a large living-room, with high, wide french windows overlooking the gardens. They were open to let in a light breeze and she stepped outside into the fresh, sweet air of a lovely summer day.

She took a long, deep breath and felt better. The gardens looked peaceful and inviting. A little exploration might help. She found a path, which wound around to the rear of the house where trees climbed a gentle hill, and began to walk. About halfway up, she saw the glint of water and remembered Jocelyn's photograph of a large luxurious swimming-pool. She turned in that direction and came upon it a moment later, sheltered on one side by leafy trees and sparkling blue against the deeper blue of the sky. There were groups of tables and chairs, with sun-loungers and multicoloured umbrellas dotted casually around the paved perimeter. It was deserted and very inviting.

The sun was hot, fanned by a light, cooling breeze. . .so unlike the bleak grey weather she'd left behind in England.

June, back home, had been cold enough for

February; a cold wet summer following in the wake of a cold wet winter, and when the company for which she worked as a secretary had gone bust and made her redundant, some latent urge for adventure had risen. It had been then she'd decided to blow much of her small hoard of redundancy money and come to America on what had promised to be the holiday of a lifetime.

She allowed herself a small, bitter smile. The holiday so far had been nothing but aggravation and, given the circumstances, could only get worse.

A faint shadow passed over the surface of the pool, interrupting her thoughts, and Jo started. Looking around, she saw nothing. The garden lay as still and empty as before. Perhaps a bird had flown across the sky above her.

She gave herself a mental shake. She was here, the day was hot and a beautiful swimming-pool lay at her entire disposal. There was no reason why she shouldn't enjoy what was available here and now and face up to the disagreeable business of tackling Lee when the time arrived.

She hadn't brought her swimsuit, but who cared? She looked around again. Nothing and no one. She was filled with a sudden heady recklessness. Before she could think twice about it, she slipped out of her dress and loose sandals and, in bra and briefs, stood poised on the pool edge.

With a lithe and graceful movement of her slim body, she dived into the pool, gasping a little as she broke surface. Heavens! It was delicious. She swam

slowly and luxuriously, closing her eyes and aban-
doning herself to the sensation of the cool, silky
water against her skin.

A faint splash disturbed her serenity and she sank
below the surface, just as hands grabbed her waist.

With water in her eyes and chlorine in her nose
and throat, she coughed and spluttered, too indignant for fear. Dashing her hand to her eyes, she
blinked them clear and came face to face with Lee.
He was smiling, his dark eyes narrowed
disconcertingly.

'My! You have changed a lot since you went
away,' he said softly. 'First, you acquire an unheard-
of taste for books, and whereas before you hated
water now, suddenly, you can swim like a fish. One
might almost say, my dear Jocelyn, that your little
trip has made a new woman of you.'

'I am not Jocelyn.' Jo almost choked on the
chlorine and her anger. 'And I'm sure you know
damned well who I am.'

'Oh, yes. . . I know,' he agreed, suddenly grim.
'Though for a while, I must admit, you had me
fooled.'

Jo shook her head. 'I wasn't trying to fool anyone.
It was your mistake. I did try to explain.'

'But not hard enough, perhaps,' he suggested
meaningfully. There was a gleam in his eye which
seemed to spell danger. 'Last night, you seemed
happy enough to let me go on thinking you were
Jocelyn.'

With grim intent, he pulled her to him, his hand
tangling in her wet hair, drawing her face relentlessly

close to his. She'd been treading water and found
herself clinging to him to keep herself afloat. His
shock appearance had taken all the strength from
her body.

'That's not true,' she denied, shaken by his per-
ception. 'You took me by surprise. . .'

'And you obviously like surprises. . .' His eye-
brows rose in a mocking challenge. 'Yes?'

But he gave her no opportunity to reply.

His hold tightened and he kissed her, his mouth
and tongue exploring hers in a way so intimate and
familiar that she began to doubt that he really did
know she wasn't Jocelyn.

The cool water had lowered her temperature. His
body was warmer than hers and she shivered in his
embrace. With a gesture that was almost protective,
he drew her closer, his arms wrapping around her as
he took her weight. His lips never left hers.
Entwined, they floated, his body beneath hers now,
supporting her, its hard masculinity proclaiming his
arousal, exciting her senses, draining away her
control.

The remembered glimpse of his naked body, the
enforced touch of her hand against him, returned
clear and sharp, adding to her churning excitement.
Her breasts, through the thin lace of her bra, made
fiery contact with the springy hair of his chest,
driving her almost to frenzy.

Lying on him this way, she could have lifted her
head at any time to break the contact, remove the
deep, searching pressure of his lips, but somehow
she couldn't. Now, she told herself fiercely. . . Do it

now! But still she held on to him. Where was the
resistance she had promised herself earlier? It would
be useless to blame chemical attraction when it was
too late.

Somehow, from somewhere, she found the
strength to push away from him. To her surprise, he
released her easily, without a struggle, emphasising,
with a cynical smile, that his hold had never detained
her.

She swam to the side and clambered out. His eyes
followed her, full of grim amusement.

Jo clenched her teeth and faced him defiantly.
'Now you know who I am, there's no point in your
cat-and-mouse game.'

Effortlessly, he lifted his muscular body from the
water and stood up beside her, the water gleaming
on his smoothly tanned skin. Vitality flowed from
him, and she felt its warmth. She found herself
struggling to hold back a tremor of response. Even
now, she found it difficult not to respond, despite
her anger. The power of the man was frightening.

His dark, searching gaze held her defiant eyes for
seemingly endless seconds, before he said coldly, 'I
thought it was you who was playing the game. I just
went along for the ride—to see how far you were
prepared to go. For a while there, I thought it might
be the whole way.'

Jo stared at him speechless, hot humiliation washing over her like a tide. If she'd been able to fool
herself, she couldn't fool him. There was nothing to
do now. . .but run. . .

'I don't think there's any point in pursuing this conversation—or in my staying.'

Wrenching her eyes from his, she scooped up her dress and sandals, but before she had time to move away he caught her arm, swinging her roughly around to face him. His touch inflamed her. The light breeze felt chill against her burning skin, making her shiver.

'I have to change,' she said, through teeth which chattered. 'I'm cold.'

He picked up a towel from a nearby chair and drew it about her shoulders, but his face held neither concern nor kindness. His eyes locked into hers, hard and granite-grey.

'OK! Let's have the truth. Why are you here?'

Jo stared uncomprehendingly. 'To visit Jocelyn,' she answered unevenly. 'Why else?'

'That's what I'm asking you,' he said unremittingly. 'Your sister ran off weeks ago with Burt Keegan—my fellow director and one-time friend. Are you telling me you didn't know?'

Jo felt dizzy, but managed to hold his gaze. 'I didn't know. Of course I didn't.' Then, as he continued to look at her accusingly, she added with a sudden spurt of anger, 'Do you think I'd spend practically every penny I have to come here if I knew Jocelyn had left you?'

'It's possible,' he said doggedly, 'if you thought it might be an investment.'

She frowned. 'Investment? I don't understand.'

'Ahh—come on! You're Jocelyn's twin! Her identical twin!' he said derisively. 'Do you mean it didn't

occur to you that I might easily fall for a replica of
what I'd lost?'

Jo almost choked on her surprise. 'You—you
think I was offering myself to you. . .in place of
Jocelyn?'

He nodded grimly. 'You were certainly offering
something.'

Before she could stop herself, her hand shot out
and made contact with his cheek, shock mixing with
her anger as she watched the red stain spreading
across his face. Her eyes widened apprehensively as
she tried to gauge his reaction.

For a moment, he looked stunned, and then he
grinned. 'Hit the bull, did I? Thanks for the confir-
mation.' He caught her wrist just as her hand came
up a second time. 'You'd better quit while you're
winning,' he said heavily, 'or I might just forget my
manners.'

Jo's breasts heaved. 'How can you forget what
you've never known?' she spat furiously.

To her surprise, he laughed, and as she tried to
drag her hand from his he caught the free hand also
in his grasp.

'So I'm no gentleman,' he said easily. 'But I'm
also no fool. And when I hold a woman in my arms,
I know I can trust my senses, even though I can't
trust the woman.' He pulled her roughly towards
him. 'I know what was happening between us last
night. . .and just now. . .What I want to know is—
why?'

Jo struggled furiously against his grasp and against

the question he was asking. She didn't know the answer. . .didn't want to know.

'There's no point in this,' she said desperately. 'Please let me go. You're hurting me.'

His frowning gaze continued to search hers, but she turned away. Slowly he released her.

Jo sighed with relief and rubbed unconsciously at her stinging wrists. 'I'll get dressed right away and just go. If you call me a taxi I'll be ready in less than an hour.'

CHAPTER FOUR

JOANNE woke with a start. She was lying on the bed, her dress and sandals still clutched to her breast; her underwear had dried on her body.

She remembered she'd cried, but couldn't now, for the life of her, remember why. Anger would have been more appropriate—hot, blazing anger at Lee Staddon's horrible insinuations. And at herself, for the way she'd laid herself open to them.

She raised herself from the bed. How long had she been there? A glance at her watch told her it was almost three hours. If Lee had been waiting for her to leave, he'd had a long wait, she thought, with an attempt at wry humour. But, already, she was regretting her outburst of temper. It would leave her alone in an unknown foreign city, with very little money to pay her way. An unnerving situation, especially to a novice traveller like herself.

Perhaps she could apologise. The sneaky thought crept into her mind, but she rejected it almost immediately. She would go through hell and high water rather than ask him to let her stay on until her plane left for home in twelve days' time.

No. She would go, as she had said, and salvage her pride.

She was in the bath when a firm knock fell on her bedroom door.

37

She sighed. At the moment, she wasn't up to seeing anyone, not even Emie or the well-meaning Sidonie. Perhaps if she kept quiet and didn't answer they would think she was asleep and go away. No second knock sounded and she relaxed, sinking deeper into the foamed and scented bath.

'I'm afraid I can't wait any longer.' Lee's dark head popped around the doorway. 'I have to go out.'

Joanne stared at him speechless.

He walked casually into the room, as though he had every right to be there, his eyes scrutinising her as though the suds didn't exist.

Jo coloured and made a foolish gesture, as though she were pulling a sheet up around her chest.

'You're covered,' he said mockingly. 'But I've got a wonderful memory.'

Furious, Jo suddenly found her voice. 'You really do think you're irresistible, don't you?'

'Not entirely.' He shrugged amiably. 'But I've had my moments. . .' His dark eyes gleamed. 'And no complaints so far.'

'Oh, spare me the details,' Jo hissed. 'I'm sure a lot of women fall for your brand of arrogant charm. Fortunately I'm not one of them.'

He smiled and came and sat on the edge of the bath, calmly reaching forward to release a damp tendril of hair which clung to her cheek. His cool fingers burned like fire.

'It seemed to me you were enjoying what we were doing together in the pool a little while ago.'

Jo caught her breath and shrank away from his

touch. He really was despicable and it was evident he intended to spare her nothing.

'Perhaps that was part of my plan,' she snapped back furiously. 'To make you fall in love. . .'

She relapsed into silence, appalled at what she'd said, wishing she had some control over her temper and her hasty tongue.

His eyes narrowed. 'Are you telling me I was right?'

'You seemed to think so.' She was probably wrong, but had she detected a hint of doubt in his voice? 'Are you admitting you might be wrong?'

'No,' he answered, sharp and implacable, and Jo thought, once again, that he could be ruthless. . .an opponent she could in no way hope to match.

He stood up and paced the floor before speaking again. 'I came to find out what you intend to do. You said you were leaving. Have you booked accommodation elsewhere?'

Jo squirmed. He'd come to make sure he was getting rid of her. It was impossible now to tell him that she'd come on the spur of the moment, with no concrete plans at all.

'That's my business.'

A grimace of impatience crossed his face. 'I assume you didn't fly all the way here on a day trip.'

'Your assumption is right,' Jo said tightly. 'I've got a two-week return flight.' She set her chin stubbornly. 'But that's my concern, not yours.'

'It's mine. . .if I choose to be concerned,' he said coolly. 'And I do. I can't allow a guest of mine to accuse me of being inhospitable.'

'Not even an unexpected and obviously suspect guest?' she derided.

He shrugged and spread his hands in a silent gesture. His silence goaded her. He was on home ground and very sure of himself.

'Don't worry.' She shook her head. 'Your character—or rather, lack of it—is your problem. I promise not to mention it to anyone.'

For a moment, he was silent, his eyes narrowed in close assessment. Then he gave a short laugh. 'Sarcasm can sometimes be amusing,' he conceded.

'I'm glad you're amused,' Jo said disdainfully. It was almost impossible to hold a sensible conversation with him. 'Now, if you don't mind, I'd like to get out of the bath.'

'Go ahead.' He folded his arms. 'Don't mind me.'

'In private.'

She heard him sigh in his throat. 'I don't have much time. If you really want to spare your modesty, then stay put and listen to what I have to say.'

Jo made a small aggravated sound. 'I don't seem to have much choice.'

He nodded. 'You don't have *many* choices, I agree. But I've come to talk to you about the ones you *do* have.'

He frowned, lines of irritation forming on his brow and along his cheeks. Even mean and moody, he exuded a subtle fascination.

He was casually dressed, the neck of his shirt open to reveal the strong column of his throat and the dark hair on his tanned and muscular chest.

Jo caught herself up and looked quickly away,

grateful that he was too engrossed to notice her appraisal.

'Unfortunately, your unexpected visit has come at an awkward time,' he went on. 'Tomorrow, I'm off on a month's vacation. I've given Emie and Sidonie that amount of time off and plan to close up the house.'

'Oh. . . I see.' Jo's heart sank. Even if she had been able to bring herself to give that apology, it wouldn't have done any good. He was obviously determined to make sure she left his house. She swallowed hard. 'Well. In that case, I'll try not to hold you up. It won't take me long to pack and I should be gone in an hour. I'll need a taxi.'

She smiled coolly to cover the small voice of panic. If the taxi fare was as expensive as the first one, she might shortly be reduced to sleeping on the streets.

Lee was nodding. 'If that's what you want. I'll be happy to fix you up with a hotel.'

Jo laughed shortly. 'I think I'd better do that. Your choice would probably bankrupt me.'

His dark, watchful eyes were on her face. 'As your host, of course, I'll take care of the cost.'

Jo sat up indignantly. 'You'll do nothing of the sort.'

The sudden movement revealed the soft swell of her breasts and Lee's darkly mocking gaze moved pointedly downwards.

She was tempted to sink down again beneath the waterline, but stifled the urge, her proud spirit revolted, both by his chauvinism and his offer.

'Don't be silly,' he said calmly. 'I can afford it—you obviously can't. It would be my pleasure.'

'I'm sure it would,' she gritted. 'In fact, you'd like nothing better than for me to take your charity. That way, you could convince yourself it really was your money I was after.' Jo glared at him, her fury growing. 'After your accusations at the pool, I wouldn't ever want to be indebted to you. . .for anything.'

He made an exasperated sound and stood up and moved to the window to stare pensively out.

Jo's eyes followed him, dwelling on the broad shoulders beneath his well-cut shirt, the firm, muscled curve of his hips and long legs in his close-fitting trousers. She felt the acceleration of her heartbeat and groaned silently.

Why was her response so automatic. . .so powerful? She didn't know. But she did know his charisma had little or nothing to do with money. If Jocelyn had gained the love of a man like Lee Staddon, why had she thrown it away?

He turned suddenly, catching her eye, and Jo hastily averted her gaze.

'Have you ever been sailing?'

The unexpected question caught her unawares. She chanced looking up. 'Not unless you count a rowing-boat on my local lake,' she answered, the hint of sarcasm hiding her inner turmoil.

She was surprised by the glimmer of amusement in his eyes.

'Well, it's a start. Did you do the rowing?'

'Of course,' she retorted, nettled by the futility of

the conversation. 'But what has that to do with anything?'

'I intend sailing my yacht on vacation.' He eyed her narrowly. 'If you won't accept a hotel, I'm prepared, as a second option, to have you aboard.' He smiled at Jo's startled and suddenly wary expression. 'I've no intention of offering you a free ride. If you come along, it would be as a working crew member. In which case, some skill with a dinghy would come in handy when bringing the yacht into harbour.'

Jo stared at him. 'You. . .you want me to. . .come sailing with you?'

'It's not a question of what I want.' He grimaced. 'It's an alternative solution to the current problem. I don't have to like it.'

He paused, waiting frowningly for some response from her. It was a long time coming, as Jo tried to work out his motives for the offer, but she could come up with nothing obvious except that he might still be trying to test *her* motives. But why would he bother, when he could justifiably disown any responsibility for her? There was no way she could answer that yet. If she accepted his offer, no doubt she would find out.

From her own point of view, if she turned him down the alternative was to hang around alone in the cheapest room she could find, waiting for her return flight to the cold grey skies of home.

'Well—what do you say?' he prompted impatiently.

Jo chewed her lip and looked at him doubtfully.

He was manipulating her in some way, that was
certain, but, all the same, she couldn't suppress a
sudden surge of excitement. If she worked her
passage, it wouldn't be a question of taking anything
from him—she would be earning her keep.

'I might be hopeless at sailing,' she said at last.

'That's quite possible,' he agreed drily. 'But I'll
let Moray Delaney, my second-in-command, worry
about that. He has responsibility for the crew.' He
gave a short laugh. 'I dare say he'll manage to keep
you busy.'

Jo snorted silently. It was obvious that, once
aboard, he intended to wash his hands of her. Well,
that would suit her fine. The less she came in contact
with him and his disturbing influence, the better she
would like it.

'I. . . I don't know what to say,' she said, still
doubtful.

'It's a reasonable offer,' he replied shortly, with
an irritable shrug of his broad shoulders. 'Just take
it or leave it.'

Jo saw Lee the following morning at breakfast. After
a sleepless night, she had woken tired and heavy,
wondering whether he was still determined to take
her sailing.

He was in the dining-room before her and looked
up as she entered. His expression was withdrawn,
his manner polite and cool. He was probably blaming her for the fact that he felt obliged to take her
along with him on his holiday. It was obvious he

though she were a cheap imitation of her sister, begging for the crumbs she left behind?

'Thank you, but I'd rather you didn't,' she replied stiffly. 'You might find it hard to believe, but I have clothes enough to suit my taste—I don't need your hand-outs.'

His dark eyes glinted angrily into her blazing blue ones. 'Then give them to some charity that does. They're worth a small fortune.'

Thin-lipped, Jo continued to glare at him. 'I'd rather leave that to you. They're your problem—not mine.'

She saw his hands clench and he took a step towards her, anger grooving deeply into his handsome face. Involuntarily, she stepped back. Her heart began pounding in her ears and she found herself holding her breath. Had she gone too far? Was he going to hit her?

He gripped her shoulders and shook her. 'Dammit—you're the most infuriating. . .'

Jo tried to wrench herself away. She shouldn't be feeling this flaring excitement. Her hands should be itching to hit his imperious face, not longing to smooth the angry lines from his cheeks.

He held her more tightly, pulling her struggling body against his, the tensile strength of his fingers more binding than any steel. Jo's resistance began to ebb and she found herself wishing, treacherously, that he was holding her with a different kind of passion.

His face was too close, his mouth a breath away. If he moved a fraction more, their lips would meet.

Jo's nerves jumped erratically. Was he going to kiss her?

Dark and intimidating, his eyes bored into hers, searching for weakness. Jo wondered how much longer she could hold out.

'You can please yourself about the clothes,' he gritted, tight-lipped. 'If you're trying to impress me——'

'Impress you!' Jo burned with fury. 'Why should I try to do that?' She smiled maliciously. 'You're impressive enough for both of us. . .this beautiful house, more money than you know what to do with, your own yacht to sail away from all the little worries I'm sure must go with wealth. How could I possibly compete——?'

'You're right,' he broke in harshly. 'You couldn't.'

He shook her roughly free, so that she stumbled back towards the bed. Her knees buckled and she sat down heavily, the fire of outrage that had been shooting through her veins doused by the look of glittering, cold dislike he shot her.

'You'll come sailing,' he gritted forcefully, 'but, from now on, I think it might be better for both of us if you kept out of my way.'

Jo silently agreed with him, but wondered how it was going to be possible aboard a yacht at sea.

CHAPTER FIVE

'MORAY DELANEY!' Lee called across to a tall, shaggy-haired man who stood on the quayside talking to a leggy blonde. 'Come over here and give a hand.'

'Lee! Well, hi!' The tall man turned and grinned. 'I've been wondering where you'd got to.' Jo watched as he leaned to kiss the young girl lightly. 'Take care, honey. See you soon.'

The blonde's pouting look of disappointment changed to interest as she saw the gleaming open car and Lee's lithe frame bending to remove the baggage from the boot.

'Who's your friend?' she asked silkily. 'He's cute.'

'He's the guy who pays my wages, honey.' Mo turned her round and gave her backside a gentle push. 'Scat! I've got work to do.'

'You certainly have,' Lee agreed sourly as Mo joined him in removing the baggage. 'This is Joanne,' he introduced Jo shortly, with a wave of his lean hand. 'She's sailing with us.'

Mo's raised brows spoke volumes of surprise, but he merely grinned and swallowed Jo's hand in his huge grip.

'Glad to have you aboard.'

Which was more than could be said for Lee, Jo observed silently, as she glanced at his closed face.

He looked as though he'd just swallowed a dose of very nasty medicine.

With an irritable gesture, he pulled the last bag from the boot and slammed it shut. 'Take her aboard now while I put the car away. She'll be crewing, but will need a little tuition from you to get started.'

Jo looked doubtfully into Mo's cheerful, open face.

'More than a little, I'm afraid,' she said apologetically. 'I've never sailed before.'

The big man lifted his shoulders in a shrug. 'No problem. Come on in.'

Jo clambered across the short gangplank that spanned the gap from the quayside to a gleaming yacht tied up alongside.

She followed Mo as Lee disappeared in the car. She was filled with hollow misgiving. Throughout the long journey down, he'd spoken little and Jo could see from his unbending expression that he was determined to do as he'd said and keep the distance between them.

And she was quite happy about that, she told herself firmly, as she clambered awkwardly down the narrow wooden steps in Mo's wake. It was just that. . .it would be nice if. . .she sighed. Perhaps she just wanted life easy for a change.

The yacht was smaller than she had expected. A sleek forty-two-footer, as Mo informed her, with compact, functional accommodation. Whether Lee liked it or not, they would certainly be living cheek by jowl for the next ten days or so.

Jo was surprised at the lack of ostentation. She'd

expected something very luxurious—more in keeping with Lee's obviously expensive tastes. Perhaps
he was down to his last million and counting the
pennies, she thought nastily.

'Your cabin's in here.'

Through the panelled lounge, which also housed
the dining area and a small galley, Mo led Jo into a
small room containing two bunks.

'My cabin's the one to the rear of the bathroom,'
Mo said, 'and Lee has the en suite master bedroom
for'ard.'

'Which bunk is mine?' Jo asked tentatively, wondering if she was expected to share.

Mo shrugged. 'Either one. They're both vacant
for the moment.'

Jo nodded and wondered if 'for the moment'
meant someone else was coming aboard later.

As though he read her thoughts, Mo continued, 'I
was arranging for an extra crew member through the
agency when Lee wired to say you were coming.
That probably won't be necessary now.'

Jo coloured. 'I wasn't being modest just now. I
really don't know the first thing about sailing. What
will you do if I'm useless?'

Mo grinned. 'You won't be.'

Lee's large bulk loomed suddenly in the doorway.
'When you've finished here come up on deck for a
briefing.'

Jo wondered if he was including her in the order.
Was she to be treated like a normal crew member,
or as an unwanted visitor?

It was obviously going to be the latter, she thought

resentfully, as Lee caught Mo's eye and jerked his head upwards towards the deck.

'Make yourself at home.'

He threw the words casually over his shoulder to Jo, leaving her in no doubt that she was excluded from the intended tête-à-tête. He was obviously going to fill Mo in on his irksome situation with his uninvited guest and didn't want her around to hear his version of the purpose of her visit.

She boiled with indignation, but said nothing. If she was going to rise to every piece of bait he threw her way, she'd have her work cut out and things were going to be difficult enough without that.

'Don't mind me,' she said sweetly.

Deliberately, she set about the task of unpacking her few belongings in the deep drawers and small wardrobe. When the holdall was empty, she folded it flat and stored it in the narrow cupboard above the bunk. Now she could actually see the storage space aboard, she understood Lee's concern about her case. There was literally no place in which it could have been easily and safely accommodated. So he had not, as she had half suspected, been deliberately obstructive. Still, he might have been a little less irritable about explaining it to her.

At least Mo seemed glad of her company, she consoled herself, and if he wasn't influenced by Lee's biased account of her presence aboard, then his good-natured acceptance might make her stay bearable.

In the event, she needn't have worried. In the days that followed, it became obvious that Lee had delivered her into Mo's sole charge and washed his own hands of her. He spoke to her civilly enough when he had to, but his eyes seemed always to look straight through her, as though mentally denying her presence could make her disappear.

Well, unfortunately for them both, it wasn't possible for her to disappear, so they would just have to make what they could of it. For her part, Jo would gladly have met him halfway if he had showed the smallest sign of being willing to do the same, and she found herself wishing sadly that he would. But she might just as well have wished for the moon.

Mo had taken her on in his good-natured way, patiently explaining to her the rudiments of sailing. And she'd been a good student, even if she did say so herself. Mo said it too, marvelling aloud when she managed to avoid a nasty collision coming into harbour. She'd anticipated the danger and had fended off strongly, the way Mo had taught her. Lee hadn't responded to Mo's praise of her and it was obvious he didn't care a damn one way or the other.

The yacht rose and fell in a sudden swell and Jo's stomach gave a little lurch but settled back quickly. Two days ago, she'd been praying silently for the yacht to pull into harbour and remain there forever to allow her poor stomach to find its accustomed place in her body once more. She'd been so sick.

Lee had relented sufficiently to go below and find her a phial of pills.

'Take two of these as soon as you wake each morning,' he'd ordered coolly, his dark eyes flicking over her pale face, but there had been no pity in their depths. 'They should be working by the time we're ready to lift anchor.'

She'd done as he had said and today she felt fine.

From her vantage-point on the after-deck, she could see Lee now without too much risk of his seeing her. He had his back to her as he swung the wheel to change course. She watched, with reluctant fascination, the play of taut muscle beneath the tanned skin of his arms and shoulders, the strength of his lean brown hands.

She sighed. If only his personality matched his fantastic good looks, she thought wistfully. She didn't know how he'd managed it the past two days, but he had. Despite the fact that the yacht was much smaller than she'd expected, he had managed to keep out of her way, staying aloof even in the intimate confines of the main cabin.

She sighed again and straightened out the wrinkles in her blanket, moving deeper into the shade of the makeshift awning Mo had thoughtfully erected for her to sunbathe under. The sun was fierce, but the cooling breeze made it bearable. The white sails flapped above her head, dazzling against the deep blue of the sky. It wouldn't be hard to get to like this life, she told herself, with a flash of wry humour.

The boat lurched suddenly and listed as Lee turned the bow to change direction.

'Mo!' he called sharply. 'Come and take the wheel.'

Mo, who had been looping the heavy ropes, called

warps, to store in the lazarette, dropped them quickly on to the deck and moved forward to the cockpit.

'Trouble?'

'Something to starboard. I want to take a look.' Lee lifted the heavy binoculars from around his neck and trained them on the sea. 'Turn in,' he commanded urgently.

Jo stood up, made curious by the tone of his voice.

Lee's head came around as she rose. 'Come here!' he commanded. 'I want you to see this.'

Jo's pride rebelled. Come here. . .and he expected her to jump to attention. Why couldn't he speak pleasantly—smile once in a while? Her spirit wanted to ignore him, but curiosity drove her forward to stand alongside, her eyes drawn to his strong, remote profile. It gave her a funny, empty feeling, as though something was just beyond her reach.

He continued to peer through the glasses, ignoring her presence.

'What am I supposed to be looking at?' she demanded in sudden irritation, adding with heavy sarcasm, 'Or am I not allowed to ask?'

He took the glasses from his eyes and put them to hers, his arms hooking around her shoulders, holding her within their circle. It was all she could do to repress the shudder his touch aroused. She was fiercely, painfully aware of him and she wished unhappily that she wasn't. With an effort, she wrenched her attention back to the sea.

He was adjusting the lenses and, as her eyes grew accustomed, she saw the dark triangles breaking the surface of the water.

'Shark!' she cried, horrified, and recoiled against him, clutching at his forearms.

'Not shark,' Lee grunted disgustedly, but made no move to push her away. 'Don't you recognise dolphins when you see them?'

Jo's horror turned to excitement. 'Dolphins?' she shrieked. 'Real ones?'

Lee's laugh held genuine amusement. 'Real's the only kind there is.'

A strange thrill shot through her. 'Are you sure? I can't believe it.'

'Then take a closer look.' Lee angled the lenses of the binoculars.

Through the clear green waters she could see outlined two sleek dark shapes, one a smaller replica of the other, and moving in complete unison through the bow waves.

'Oh! Look!' she cried in wonder. 'Do look, Lee! I think it's a mother and baby.'

She took the glasses from her eyes and handed them to him.

He moved away from her, closer to the rail, and adjusted the lenses to his eyes. 'There's half a dozen of them.' His voice was detached. The moment of unselfconscious closeness had passed.

'Mo,' he called, 'they're dropping back. Turn around. If they're resting, we might get to go in with the camera.'

'Aye, aye, skipper.' Mo's white grin flashed.

Jo turned startled eyes in his direction and he winked. 'You're not going into the water with them, are you?' she asked incredulously.

Mo's grin widened. 'Sure. That's what we're here for.'

Lee went below and came back up on deck with a camera and some wet suits. Mo shut off the engine and took up one of the suits.

'If you want to come in,' Lee said, tossing one of the garments towards her, 'there's a suit which should fit you.'

Jo's eyes widened. 'I wouldn't have the first idea of how to get into one of those things.' She shook her head. 'Besides. . . I don't think I'll go in. I haven't got the nerve.'

Lee was already zipping up. 'Funny,' he said. 'That's something I thought you had plenty of.'

He was bending to push his feet into flippers. She couldn't see his face, so it was impossible to tell how he'd meant that, but Jo knew it was unlikely to be a compliment.

'You're not short of gall yourself,' she retaliated through clenched teeth.

As he looked up, she was surprised to see he was grinning.

He said, 'Thanks.' And went over the side.

Mo quickily followed, leaving Jo to watch as they cut smoothly through the water to where the dolphins were swimming slowly close to the surface.

She took up the binoculars to follow their progress and, as Lee and Mo disappeared into the blue of a gently rolling swell, Jo felt suddenly bereft. She was missing out on the experience of a lifetime.

Almost without thought, she laid the glasses aside and found herself slipping into the cool waters, conscious only of a wonderful elation as she dipped beneath the water, swimming smoothly towards the dolphins and the two men, whose full attention was on the filming.

Even before she had reached the group, the creatures seemed to have sensed her approach. Mother and baby eyed her closely and then suddenly the baby detached itself and came swiftly towards her.

Jo stifled a gasp, which would have filled her lungs with water. Keeping calm, she swam slowly upwards towards the surface, mercifully not too far away. Breaking the surface, she took a deep breath and steadied her nerves. The baby had meant her no harm, she reminded herself. Dolphins were supposed to be friendly creatures and very inquisitive.

Something touched fleetingly against her feet and she could see the sleek black body of the baby just below the water. This time, she couldn't prevent a gasp, which was half fright and half delight. It hadn't gone away, but had come in for a closer look.

Quickly, she took a breath and submerged. The baby had turned back towards her, moving close to nudge her thigh. The contact was gentle and the creature's bright eye seemed full of fun. Jo longed to touch the gleaming body, but resisted the urge.

At that moment, the mother moved purposefully towards her baby and Jo's heart began to pound with fright. Here, in the water, the dolphin was far larger than she had imagined. Her lungs were bursting and she wanted desperately to breathe air, but some instinct warned her to stay put.

She almost suffocated as the creature came near, but the long snout only nudged the baby away, and together they swam back to the other dolphins.

Jo waited two more seconds before surfacing. Her lungs burned fiercely as the cool air rushed in, and her nerve for excitement seemed to have vanished. A mixture of fear and elation lent strength to her limbs as she swam back towards the yacht. But her body weighed like lead as she struggled to pull herself aboard.

For a moment, she was grateful for the strong push from behind, which sent her shooting up and over the rail, to land in an untidy heap on the deck, but gratitude turned to outrage as Lee towered menacingly above her.

He tore his mask from his face, which was red with fury. 'What the hell did you think you were doing?' he demanded as Jo glared back at him, all pleasure gone.

'These aren't your Marineland dolphins, you know. They're wild and unpredictable. Chances are none of them have ever seen a human being before. Going in the way you did—messing with the baby— you could have got yourself killed.'

'I wasn't messing with anything,' Jo retorted hotly. 'It came to see me. I couldn't help that.'

'You could help being there in the first place,' Lee growled. 'If you'd said you wanted to go in, Mo or I would have got you into suitable gear and kept an eye out for you.'

'I don't need your permission to do anything,' Jo retorted, scrambling up from her ungainly sprawl. 'I'm not your responsibility.'

'Hmph!' Lee snorted. 'So I keep telling myself.' His eyes swept disparagingly over her and he touched a place on her waist and the top of her leg. 'You're bruised,' he pronounced frowningly. 'Probably from contact with the baby. Underwater, you wouldn't feel the impact.'

'Maybe not,' Jo argued hotly. 'But I certainly felt the impact of the deck when you pushed me. If I'm bruised from anything—then it's that.' She slapped irritably at his hand, which was still massaging the purpling area on her leg. 'I'm perfectly capable of looking after myself, thank you.'

He laughed unpleasantly and straightened. 'After this idiotic episode, I'd be a fool to believeyou.'

'You don't need my help to make you into a fool,' Jo cried, angrily. She rearranged her bikini, which was presently leaving little to the imagination, and dragged her hair over her shoulder to wring the water from it. 'You're quite good at managing that yourself.'

Jo heard Mo's explosive laugh as she turned away to go below.

'That kid doesn't miss a trick,' she heard him say. 'Added to that. . .she's got a hell of a lot of guts.'

Jo looked back furtively to see Lee's face. It was grim.

'I wish she had as much common sense,' he said. 'Then perhaps we could all relax.'

Jo slammed the cabin door.

CHAPTER SIX

AFTER dinner, Jo played chess with Mo.

Lee sat alone on the forward deck, moodily drawing on a thin cigar.

'I've never seen Lee smoke before,' she remarked in surprise.

'He rarely does,' Mo responded. 'But he *always* does when he's got something heavy on his mind.'

Jo wondered silently what was weighing so heavy. Her eyes kept straying involuntarily to him, distracting her from her game.

'You know what?' Mo said suddenly. 'It's my guess you're kinda fond of that guy.'

Jo flushed. 'I don't know why you should think that. As a matter of fact, he's the most infuriating man I've ever met: self-opinionated, bigoted——'

'Aw, come on, honey!' Mo patted her hand. 'He's maybe a man who's had his share of let-downs.'

Jo bit her lip, feeling guilty again, but also resentful. 'I know my sister let him down,' she said. 'But I'm beginning to think she might not have been entirely at fault.'

He nodded amicably. 'Sure. Every story has two sides.'

His tone dismissed the subject, and he turned his attention back to his next move, but Jo couldn't concentrate and all but threw the game away. There were questions in her mind that needed answering.

'You said "let-downs", plural,' she said as Mo wryly collected up the pieces. 'Was there someone else who let Lee down, besides Jocelyn?'

Mo's open face closed suddenly. 'Now, that's some question, young lady.'

'I know, but it's not just idle curiosity.' Jo coloured faintly. 'You know Lee so well and I really do want to understand him. At the moment, that's not too easy.' She touched his arm coaxingly. 'Can't you tell me a little bit about him?'

Mo's eyes probed hers and then he shrugged.

'Lee and I were at college together. From totally different backgrounds, of course, but we shared the same broken-down apartment. Lee was going through a phase I guess a lot of rich kids go through—blaming money for all the troubles of the world and making out like he could get along without it.'

He paused reflectively. 'His mother was alive then and I guess she thought he would grow out of it, because she kind of went along with him, bringing him food parcels as if he were some kind of refugee.' He grinned. 'We ate them and generally just had a lot of fun.'

Jo smiled. 'I can imagine.' She found herself wishing she had known Lee in those days and hastily squashed the thought. 'Then what happened?' she prompted.

'Then Cyndi happened.' He sighed. 'I met her first, in a snack bar where she was working to help pay her way through college. For a while, we had a little something going. . .nothing too heavy. Then, one day, I introduced her to Lee.'

He looked towards Lee, who had his head back and his eyes closed. Jo followed his gaze. Lee's profile looked sternly handsome in repose.

'I should have known better, I guess.' Mo shrugged. 'There was no contest. She fell for Lee hook, line and sinker.' He tweaked Jo's nose playfully. 'That's an old nautical expression.'

Jo laughed. 'I know.'

It was hard to tell if Mo resented losing his girl to Lee. Jo thought he probably did.

'Did Lee feel the same way?' she asked, consumed with curiosity.

'Sure. I think he admired her for her guts as much as for her looks. You know. . .working her way through college, doing it all off her own bat, without money—all that stuff!'

'She must have been some girl,' Jo said, sounding a little cynical.

'Yeah.' Mo's eyes gleamed with understanding humour. 'Things went along OK for quite a while. They shared the same ideas about money, politics, parents. They even discussed what it would be like to get hitched—two living as cheaply as one— something like that.'

'Oh!' Jo was jolted. Somehow, she hadn't imagined Lee as having been married and divorced. For some strange reason, she didn't like the idea. 'And did they? Get married, I mean.'

'Cyndi did. . .but not to Lee.' He laughed at Jo's

puzzled expression. 'Lee's father went ill, and Lee had to take time off. . .a couple of months—three or four, maybe. When he got back Cyndi had gone. She'd packed up her studies to marry some guy who was loaded with dough.'

'Oh, poor Lee.' Jo's heart went out in sympathy to the young man of ideals who'd been dealt such a blow. 'It must have hurt him badly.'

'Yeah,' Mo agreed. 'I guess so.' He was assembling the chess pieces in readiness for another game. 'Which do you want?'

'No, thanks.' Jo shook her head. 'I feel a bit too restless to concentrate. Mo, finish the story, please.'

Mo shrugged. 'There's not much more to tell. Lee's father died that year and, when Lee graduated, he took over the business. He's done pretty well at it.'

'Making money,' Jo observed critically.

'Well, sure.' Mo sounded amused. 'Nobody's in business to make a loss.'

Jo snorted softly. 'So there wasn't that much difference between Cyndi and himself after all. I'm willing to bet that if they had married, they would have made a fine couple.'

'Maybe. Who knows?' Mo spread his hands.

Jo chewed at her bottom lip, silently following her own train of thought. A sad, disillusioning affair for a young man, but surely it hadn't set his mind in rigid distrust of the opposite sex for the rest of his life? There must have been others capable of building up his trust again.

'And after Cyndi,' she prompted at last.

'After Cyndi,' Mo repeated, 'Lee made sure the women he went with were the kind who made no secret of their liking for money. . .and he gave them plenty.'

And gave himself no chance of finding real love, Jo mused wryly. She thought suddenly of the racks of expensive clothes hanging in Jocelyn's bedroom wardrobe.

'And I suppose he included Jocelyn in that category?' She sounded belligerent and Mo jumped back in mock horror, his hands raised as though to protect himself. 'Then why was he proposing to marry her?'

'Don't ask me, honey. Ask the man himself.'

Jo subsided and found herself studying Lee again. She wished she could ask him. . .and vowed one day she would.

Mo collected up the chess pieces, folded the board and placed them carefully into the lacquered box.

'Why don't we go for a stroll around the harbour?' he suggested. 'If you're restless, you won't sleep in this heat. And the exercise will do you good.'

He hadn't spoken loudly, but Lee suddenly stirred. Jo wondered if he'd heard and worried he'd also been able to hear what she and Mo had been discussing. But he simply adjusted his position in the chair and settled himself again.

Mo stood up and pulled her to her feet. 'I know a nice quiet little bar where we can get a cool drink. Sound good?'

'Yes. Lovely.' Jo hesitated, her glance stealing to

Lee's still figure. 'Should we invite Lee?' she asked uncertainly.

'Certainly not.' Mo grinned. 'Three's a crowd. A cliché, but true none the less.' He took her hand and led her across the deck. 'We're off for a stroll,' he called cheerfully to Lee as he lifted Jo down on to the quay. 'And you wouldn't want to play goose-berry, would you, Lee?' Without waiting for a reply, he grasped Jo's hand again and walked her away from the yacht.

In the growing dusk, the lights were on all along the harbour, illuminating the assortment of yachts bobbing gently on the calm water. People sat eating or drinking on the decks, or gossiped in small groups, comparing notes and boasts about their crafts. It all looked very slow-paced and affluent.

How the other half lives, Jo mused, feeling sud-denly as though she'd been caught up in some kind of fairy-tale. The skies back home were probably cloudy, full of threatening rain, and here she was in the balmy warmth of a brilliant evening, strolling hand in hand with a tall, handsome man. A fairy-tale indeed, except that the handsome man wasn't the prince of her dreams.

He was back on the yacht, with an expression on his face like a thunder-cloud. Jo hadn't been able to resist looking over her shoulder at Lee as they strolled away and was shocked by the look he had thrown after them. He obviously couldn't bear for her even to spend a pleasant hour in the company of someone who didn't resent her presence, she thought angrily.

She looked up into Mo's smiling, open countenance and felt wistful. Why couldn't she fall for someone like him—warm, kind and uncomplicated?

They ate fresh crab and cress sandwiches and drank ice-cold beer in a small, spartan bar on the far side of the quay. Jo was surprised by the hard wooden chairs and scrubbed tables, but the fashionably dressed sailing fraternity seemed very much at home there. Perhaps people with too much affluence sometimes hankered for a little reminder of how lucky they were, Jo mused a little spitefully.

Mo told her tall stories about his sailing exploits, interspersed with humorous and sometimes malicious tales of the people who came and went in the bar. Some of them made her laugh out loud, drawing the glances of some of the men close by. Frank admiration shone in male eyes and, though she averted her glance quickly, it made her feel good.

They strolled back to the *Ilona* more than two hours later, both a little tipsy. The beer had been strong and Jo had swallowed down thirstily the first two glasses. The third she had sipped, refusing a fourth, but her head felt light, her body more relaxed than she could remember being in a long while.

At the door of her cabin, Mo bid her a ceremonious good night with a smacking kiss on her hand and a light, laughing brush of his lips against hers.

'Farewell, Princess,' he said dramatically. 'Beyond the pearly dawn of the morrow, we shall meet again.'

Jo laughed. 'You're drunker than I thought.'

'Yes. But only on love,' he answered in the same throbbing tones.

Jo blinked, caught by an intonation, but seeing the suddenly wary expression in her eyes Mo grinned.

'Didn't know I had a career in acting, did you?'

'No.' Jo relaxed. 'Were you in films?'

'Yeah.' Mo's grin widened. 'Kind of. I once was on TV in a commercial for cigarettes.'

'Really?' Jo was impressed.

'No. Nearly,' Mo said. 'I failed the audition.'

'You clown,' Jo laughed.

'Now that's a job I haven't auditioned for,' he said seriously. 'Maybe with that I'd have better luck.'

He stole another light kiss before leaving Jo light-headed with laughter and the strong beer.

But, strangely, it didn't make her drowsy. In spite of her efforts to put Lee to the back of her mind, he kept surging into her consciousness along with the story of his broken romance.

Of course, she could sympathise with his disillusion, but that gave him no right to generalise about women and put them all in the same mercenary class as Cyndi.

Had Lee's attitude been one of the reasons for Jocelyn leaving him? she wondered. If so, then possibly their relationship could still be patched up. It was obvious Lee still felt an attraction for Jocelyn—feelings he'd mistakenly demonstrated to herself before he realised his error—but they were none the less real.

Nothing had ever felt so real to her, she thought guiltily.

The thought brought back vividly the sensations of his body against hers. . .the unwilling excitement of her hand held against him. Jo was filled with self-disgust. How was it possible to feel such an instant and overwhelming response to her sister's fiancé? It was nothing short of treachery.

If their parting had been due to a misunderstanding and it was possible somehow to pave the way to a reconciliation, Jo vowed she would do it. It wouldn't be easy to break through Lee's resentment, but she would try.

The resolve, however, brought a new restlessness. If only she could just speak to him. . .friend to friend. . .

In the small cabin it was airless and hot and, as Mo had predicted, she found it impossible to sleep. Giving up the struggle, she got up to fetch a cool drink from the fridge.

In the galley there was a light, cool breeze blowing down from the deck and, after pouring her drink from the can into a glass, she made her way up.

The sky was clear; the faint pearly grey light of dawn Mo had spoken of so dramatically was beginning low on the horizon. Soon it would turn yellow and the sun would begin to appear.

Jo leant on the rail and sighed. 'Lord! This is beautiful!' she spoke softly aloud to herself, because there was no one with whom she could share the moment, adding with a burst of irritation, 'So, how do we contrive to make life so petty and small?'

'Dawn was always a philosophical time of day.'

Lee's amused voice startled her and she spun around.

'Do you mind not creeping up on me like that?' she snapped, embarrassed to be caught talking to herself. How had he managed to be so stealthy?

In the pale light, his face looked mysterious; all planes and angles. His eyes gleamed but his mouth didn't smile.

'Last time it was you who crept up on me.'

Jo coloured, remembering what had followed her awakening of him in the study. 'Yes,' she admitted softly. 'The early hours of the morning seems to be our favourite time for meeting.'

He came to stand beside her at the rail. 'What's the matter? Couldn't you sleep?'

'No.' She felt his nearness like an electrical current, its tingling effect coursing through her whole body. 'The cabin was too hot.'

'Yeah. That's why I sometimes prefer to sleep up here on deck.' His tone was low and friendly and Jo felt herself relaxing. 'Bare. . .in a bag. . .on the hard boards. You should try it some time. You might enjoy it.'

Jo looked at him, surprised by the twinkle in his dark eyes. Was this some kind of invitation?

He was wearing a towelling robe, tied loosely at the waist, the deep V revealing the dark hairs of his muscled chest, and Jo found herself wondering if he was indeed bare beneath.

He laughed and Jo reddened. He'd obviously been aware of her scrutiny. Was he also aware of the

trend of her thoughts? she wondered in embarrassment. What was it about him that set fire to a desire
she hadn't known existed?

'It sounds more like a hardship than an enjoyment,' she said flippantly in an attempt to distract
him.

'Maybe that's the attraction.'

Jo thought again of the bar she'd been in earlier
with Mo. The hard chairs, the unadorned tables.
The symbols of hardship. A pretence of struggle.

'Perhaps that's what your life is lacking,' she said
tentatively. 'The struggle.'

His eyes appraised her coolly. 'I wasn't aware my
life lacked anything important.'

Jo bit her lip. His expression led her on to explain
herself defensively. 'I. . . I meant. . .if you knew
what it was to *need* things you couldn't have, you
might have a little more understanding of people
who have to struggle for even their most *basic*
needs.'

Lee raised his brows. 'Do I take it you speak with
the voice of experience?'

Jo coloured. 'Not exactly.'

His close, cynical scrutiny was painful to her pride.
It made her angry.

'I've had most of what I need,' she said as evenly
as she could manage, 'but obviously not everything
I ever wanted. But want is different from need.'

'I get the distinction,' he said laconically, a cool
smile playing around the corners of his mouth. 'Are
you saying I'd be a better man if there was something
I needed and couldn't have?'

Jo looked warily into his shadowed eyes. 'Is this a serious question—or sarcasm?'

He shrugged, ignoring the put-down. 'It's serious.'

Jo squared her shoulders. If he wanted the truth, she'd give it to him. 'Yes,' she said slowly. 'I think you probably would be a better man. . .for a little adversity.'

For a long moment there was silence, almost as though he was seriously considering what she had said.

'Thank you for your opinion,' he said at last, and she could tell from his tone that he had been considering nothing more serious than putting her in her place.

'Don't mention it,' she said in a low furious voice. 'But it's obvious my opinion doesn't count.'

He shrugged. 'It's academic really, isn't it?'

'Meaning you're never likely to know that kind of need?' she challenged him.

'You tell me,' he said drily. 'You're the lady with all the answers.'

'Not all the answers. There are a few I can't work out on my own.' Goaded, Jo rushed on into forbidden territory. 'For instance, why should Jocelyn leave you to go off with someone else, when all her letters to me were full of her love for you? It doesn't make sense.'

She was expecting him to be angry, but he just shrugged cynically.

'I've given up trying to make sense of women.'

'Which probably means you've never really tried,' Jo said doggedly. 'Perhaps if you'd made an effort to know Jocelyn, you might have saved your relationship with her.'

Jo caught herself up with a gasp. She hadn't meant to sound so critical—so accusing.. . .

But Lee was smiling with irritating calm. 'What's the point of attempting the impossible?' But, before she could answer, his mood had altered. 'Your sister changed like the wind. Hot and strong one minute, cold as the mountains the next.'

Jo bit her lip, startled by the sudden change and unable to find a quick retort. It was true that Jocelyn had always been changeable, but there had to be more to it than that. . .didn't there?

'I simply don't understand,' she said at last.

He moved restlessly beside her, turning so that his back leant against the rail. 'Then don't bother to try. It isn't your concern.' In this position, he stood against the light, his face only barely visible, but looking directly into hers. 'Unless, of course, you're pleading your sister's cause.'

With his fingers, he lightly brushed a stray wisp of hair from her cheek. Jo moved back from his electric touch and from the unfathomable gleam in his dark eyes.

'I'm not pleading Jocelyn's cause,' she denied quickly. 'It's just——'

His hand covered her lips, stemming the flow of her words. 'Good,' he said softly. 'Because it's a lost cause.'

Jo felt the tremor his touch engendered and was almost engulfed in panic. His power over her was unbearable and she wanted desperately to deny it.

'If there's the smallest chance you could still be happy together——'

Lee sucked in his breath—a harsh, angry sound which cut her off mid-sentence. 'For Pete's sake,' he exploded. 'The woman ran off with another man. Do you expect me to run around behind them trying to understand? Do I look that kind of a fool?'

Jo was stunned by the raw hurt in his voice—the hidden pain and anger which ran, still, so close to the surface.

'I. . . I'm sorry,' she whispered raggedly. 'I shouldn't have interfered.'

'No! Dammit! You shouldn't.' He grasped her upper arms in a grip of steel. 'Whatever it is you're trying to do to me. . .don't.'

Jo stared helplessly into his face, close enough for her to feel the warmth of his breath lifting her hair.

The pain of his grip was nothing to the torment that was tearing through her—because she wanted to open her arms to him. . .to offer him the comfort of her love to ease his heartache. But it was plain only Jocelyn could do that.

'I'm just trying to get through to you,' she said shakily. 'I wish I knew how.'

His grip loosened and he drew her suddenly into his arms. 'Honey, you do know how.'

She looked up and met his gaze, startled by the softening of the hard lines of his face, the burning intensity of his eyes.

'If you've forgotten, let me refresh your memory.'

His head dipped suddenly, his lips covering hers

searchingly as though he was seeking an answer in her response.

She wanted desperately to give him the answer she strongly suspected lay in her vulnerable heart. But she knew despairingly that only as a replica of Jocelyn could she give him one he truly wanted.

She kissed him back for a few fleeting seconds, tasting the sweetness of his lips for herself, before pushing him away. He moved back without resistance.

He looked at her searchingly, his face seeming pale in the yellow light of dawn. 'What is it?'

She wanted to tell him she was tired of her part as Jocelyn's stand-in, but the words stuck in her throat.

A look of resigned impatience crossed his face. 'Jo. Forget whatever it is you're aiming at.'

Jo's soft lower lip trembled. He was still caught in that same old mistaken rut, thinking she was trying some confidence trick.

'I'm not aiming at anything,' she answered wearily. 'If you could only recognise honesty when you see it, you'd know I was thinking of you. . .and Jocelyn.'

His fingers bit into her flesh. 'Forget it. I have.'

Liar! Jo stared at him, wanting to shout the word. How could he expect her to believe he'd forgotten? Only seconds ago, she'd seen the pain of remembering clear in his face.

His closeness forced her head up and back. Wide-eyed she stared into his face, searching for something important but elusive, the need flashing through her mind with a speed that left no memory to cling to.

'This is you and me,' he whispered, his dark eyes narrowing on hers with an intensity it was impossible to define. 'Just now, I want *you*.'

The hard pressure of his hands gave way to tenderness as they moved down to her waist, drawing her to him.

'Relax, Jo. Let it happen.'

He brushed his lips sweetly against hers and she closed her eyes, not wanting him to see her temptation.

Forget his love for Jocelyn! He hadn't meant it. It was his way of hiding the hurt.

It would be so easy to yield. . .to take what he was offering. There was no pretence in her now. She wanted him—freely. . .honestly. . .defencelessly.

But, greedily, she wanted more. She wanted him in the certainty that Jocelyn's image no longer merged with hers in his mind. His body wasn't enough. She wanted his heart.

'Let me go, Lee.'

Her heart broke as he released her.

'Goodnight.'

She turned and left him. . .before her tears told him what he must never know.

CHAPTER SEVEN

Jo WENT back to her bunk, but she couldn't sleep. Lee had wanted her and the thought was torment. Why hadn't she been able to do as he'd asked? Relax and let it happen? Somehow, it had been impossible. And she hadn't been thinking of Jocelyn this time, but of herself. Some last vestige of pride had denied her the solace of half a loaf.

Crouched miserably in her bunk, she found herself thinking that perhaps, as proverbially, it might have been better than none, but almost immediately she rejected the thought. He'd wanted her. Yes. But only to help him forget his need.

She had talked to him of unfulfilled need, imagining then that he knew nothing of it, but now the realisation hit her like a blow. He had known need. He'd needed Jocelyn, perhaps the first woman he'd learnt to trust in years, and she'd left him.

He was on deck when she finally gave up the effort to sleep and rose to make a cup of tea, and she wondered fleetingly whether he had simply stayed there after she'd left.

He turned as her head rose up through the hatch.

'Good morning,' she murmured awkwardly, wondering what he had been thinking about in the past couple of hours. Was he still resentful of her rejecting him?

It was hard to tell. He returned her greeting pleasantly enough, his eyes flicking over her face as she came to stand beside him, but his expression was unreadable.

'Is Mo about?' she asked, more to break the silence than because she wanted to know.

'He's gone ashore to pick up an extra to crew.' Lee's mouth twisted wryly. 'Don't worry! He hasn't deserted you. He'll be back about lunch.'

Jo's eyes lifted to his in surprise at his mocking tone. 'I wasn't worried,' she said defensively. 'I. . . I just wondered if he wanted a cup of tea.'

'Sure.' Lee nodded shortly. 'Well, since he's not here, how about making *me* a cup of coffee?'

'Well, of course.' Jo's surprise increased. His tone was odd, hard-edged, and if she didn't know better she might almost have thought he was jealous of her friendship with Mo. But that was ridiculous. 'You're the skipper,' she said flippantly in an unconscious effort to lighten the atmosphere, but Lee didn't respond.

'Yeah,' he said. 'Maybe, from now on, we should all just remember that.'

Feeling bewildered, Jo went below to make his coffee and, by the time she came back, he seemed perfectly composed, so that Jo wondered if her imagination had led her to read too much into the episode.

'Do you want something to eat?'

He shook his head. 'No, thanks. I've got some work to do on the log. Maybe you could clean the place up a bit while you're waiting for Mo.'

She staied after him in astonishment as he went below. She hadn't been imagining things, she told herself incredulously. He really was piqued. For some reason, she felt quite pleased.

As she scrubbed down the deck, Jo wondered why an extra crew had been necessary. Now she'd got the hang of sailing, she flattered herself that she was almost as good as a real crew member.

Mo arrived just before lunch. Jo had just finished washing off the hatches and stood up to stretch her back. Lee had come up on deck about half an hour earlier and was tidying up the warps in the lazarette. He had brought her a cup of coffee, but there had been little conversation between them.

She had opened her mouth to thank him before she thought better of it, then wondered why she was pandering to Lee's childish stupidity.

'Hi there, Jo!' Mo called cheerfully. 'I hope lunch is ready. We're starving.'

'I've been too busy to think of lunch,' she teased and heard him groan.

His appetite was enormous and it wouldn't take him long to demolish his share of the cold german sausage and thick ham she'd bought to go with the huge bowl of salad and crisp fresh rolls.

'Who's "we" anyway? Nobody told me we were expecting a newcomer.'

Mo was coming aboard followed by a shapely blonde. Where did he find them all? Jo wondered with a little shake of her head. No wonder Lee felt a little jealousy; Mo was a very attractive man and the girls around the harbours seemed to appreciate his brand of charm. But, as he'd said himself, when Lee was about there was no contest.

'Not exactly a newcomer.' Mo bent to kiss Jo's cheek. 'Stacey's crewed for us before.'

'Stacey! What are you doing here?' Lee's voice broke in behind them. 'I thought you'd given up agency crewing.'

'Hello, Lee.'

The young blonde's smile was brilliant and it was turned on full force into Lee's impassive face. 'Oh! I still go down there once in a while, just to keep my hand in.' She reached up to kiss his cheek. 'I was happy to volunteer when I saw your name in the book.' Her blue eyes gleamed invitingly. 'As I told you before, I'm available any time you need me.'

Lee coolly disentangled her hands from around his neck. 'Yeah. Well, I guess we all need you right now. We're thinking of doing some night sailing and Joanne here isn't experienced enough to take night-watch alone.'

Jo frowned. It was the first she'd heard of it, and how could he tell she wouldn't be up to taking the night-watch alone if she hadn't tried?

The girl's attention had been almost totally on Lee since her arrival. She seemed hardly to have noticed Jo's existence. Her gaze was turned fully on to her now and she quite obviously didn't like what she saw.

Jo, with her hair tied up in a scarf and with dirty water-marks on the legs of her rolled-up white trousers, was obviously going to be no competition, but she was still another woman. The theme of

Stacey's thoughts was written clearly in her express-
ive face.

'Stacey will be sharing your cabin, Jo,' Lee said.

Jo stifled a sigh. 'I thought she might be.' She held
out her hand in a friendly gesture. 'Welcome aboard.
Would you like me to show you the way?'

The girl's eyes were chips of blue ice. 'Thanks,
but I don't need your help. I already know my way
about this boat—every inch from stem to stern.'
Pointedly ignoring Jo's outstretched hand, she
brushed regally past. 'Mo, bring my bag.'

'Sure.' Mo reached down good-naturedly, but
Lee's hand restrained him.

'This is no hotel, Stacey,' he said coolly. 'And
Mo's no bell-boy. If you're too frail to manage your
own bag, you'll be no good as a crew.'

His eyes held Stacey's outraged glare.

'You know I'm the best they have down at the
agency. I was sailing almost before I could walk.'

'Fine.' Lee nodded. 'And that's what you're here
for. Make sure you remember.'

Stacey's colour deepened to angry red, but it was
Jo she sought to deliver a look of pure dislike. 'Oh!
I get it!' Her eyes lashed up and down Jo's untidy
form. 'Can't say I care for the new entertainment.'

Jo watched with suddenly bated breath as Lee
clenched his fists and advanced a step towards
Stacey.

'Anything else you don't care for, Stacey, just let
me know. I'd be happy to put you ashore.'

For long seconds their eyes locked in silent battle
and then Stacey sighed.

'I guess I'm just tired. You'll have to excuse me.' She picked up her bag and went below.

Jo went down to the cabin later. Stacey was in there unpacking her clothes and she'd removed Jo's few belongings from the deep drawers and thrown them on to her bunk.

'I need more space for my stuff,' she said in answer to Jo's questioning look.

Jo felt her temper flare. 'I would have moved them if you'd asked,' she said as calmly as she could, though she boiled inside.

'You weren't here to ask, so I just went ahead,' Stacey answered coolly. 'There's plenty of space in the end cupboard for what you have here.'

Jo wanted to ask her rudely why she hadn't used it, but bit her tongue. There was tension enough aboard already without adding to it with childish squabbles.

'I'll put my things away myself when you've finished.'

She went to find a clean cloth to add a little extra sparkle to the hatches and narrow side-windows. The hard rubbing gradually dispersed her pent-up fury and she took the time to give herself a little pep talk.

The next week obviously wouldn't be easy, but she would just have to make the best of it. Sharing a cabin with Stacey was going to be difficult but hopefully not impossible and, if she had to swallow a little pride now and then, it would be preferable to taking on the battle Stacey would be obviously only too happy to engage in.

Jo wondered when it was that the girl had last crewed with Lee. Her promise of availability had been blatant and open to only one interpretation. Had Lee taken her up on it while he was engaged to Jocelyn? Were other women the reason Jocelyn had left? For the moment, there was no answer to that, but the question depressed Jo.

She'd moved on to Lee's windows now and she could see him in his cabin, seated at his desk, his dark head bent over the logs. Just the very sight of him started the tremor inside. The strong, tanned neck with the thick springy dark hair waving slightly at the nape did strange things to her emotions. She had never before met a man who made her long to touch him. It made her fingers itch.

Probably the dust, she told herself, deciding to leave the windows in case he looked up and saw her staring down at him.

The cabin door opened and Stacey came in, confidently, as though it was something she'd done often before. Lee didn't look up and she went to him and put her fingers in his hair, bent her lips to kiss his neck.

Jo felt the sick twisting of jealousy. Only seconds before she had been longing to do the same thing.

Lee moved his head to shrug her away and, as he turned, Stacey claimed his lips. He let her kiss him for a while, and then pushed against her shoulders.

'What's the matter?' Stacey's petulant voice reached Jo. 'Don't you like to say hello any more?'

'Sure. Hello.'

'Oh, Lee, baby.' Her lips, pouting, were very inviting.

Lee sighed. 'Stacey, all that was a long time ago. Things change.'

The girl's pout turned into a frown of frustration. 'I haven't changed.'

'I'm sure you haven't.' Lee's laugh was dry.

'What's that supposed to mean?' she demanded hotly and Jo saw Lee's hard face soften momentarily.

'Just back off, Stacey. This trip I'm not interested.'

'Oh, I see.' Stacey's face turned dull red and, even at this angle, Jo could see the flare of temper in her eyes. 'Well, maybe what you are interested in is that little deck-scrubber with her smudged make-up and cheap clothes.'

'No. You haven't changed, Stacey. Still the same spit-mouthed little hellcat.' Lee's dark brows lowered. 'Joanne is Jocelyn's twin, over here on a visit—nothing more than that—end of story.'

'Jocelyn's twin!' Stacey gasped. 'Lord! I thought there was something familiar. . .' Her face twisted suddenly. 'And don't give me that stuff about nothing between you. I know that look of yours. What are you after, Lee? An action replay?'

Lee stood up, towering over her, his face dark with fury. 'You're treading on dangerous ground, Stacey,' he warned icily. 'I suggest you quit now. You're here to crew and so is Joanne, and that, where I'm concerned, is as far as it goes for both of you.'

Jo gasped and then pulled back quickly, fearful the two below might have caught sight of her eavesdropping.

That wasn't what he'd said last night. Last night he'd wanted to make love to her. And, whether he liked it or not, Stacey had been right. What he had wanted was a rerun of his broken romance with Jocelyn.

They said eavesdroppers heard no good of themselves, and it was true. Her heart was hammering with tight fury. Thank heaven she hadn't given in to him or to her own treacherous heart.

The atmosphere on board that evening was anything but light. Mo, as usual, set out the chess-board and Jo sat down to join him. Lee sat up on the forward deck with a book and Stacey prowled the yacht like a caged tiger, holding a portable tape recorder which blasted out the latest pop music. She stopped in front of Mo and rotated her shapely curves in time to the rhythm.

'Doesn't anybody around here dance any more?' she complained petulantly.

Mo looked up, his eyes lighting in obvious appreciation of what she was displaying for him, but he just grinned. 'Keep it for later. I'm busy just now.'

Stacey tossed her blonde head at him and flounced across to Lee. 'Dance with me, Lee.'

She put the recorder down on the table, removed Lee's book from his hand and tried to pull him to his feet.

'Aw, come on, Lee. You used to like to dance.'

'I still do,' he said, resisting her efforts to drag him to his feet. 'But only when I choose to.'

The music stopped and changed to a slow, romantic number.

'There,' Stacey cried triumphantly. 'You like this one—remember?'

Suddenly, to Jo's surprise, Lee gave in.

With a sigh of resignation, he allowed himself to be pulled to his feet and, as Stacey triumphantly wound her arms about his neck, he relaxed and drew her close, his dark head against her blonde curls.

They danced to a few numbers before Lee, with a look of sudden impatience, indicated he'd had enough. 'I think I need to stretch my legs ashore.'

The girl's face brightened and she ran a slim hand through her hair. 'Give me a minute to tidy up and I'll come with you.'

Lee shook his head. 'I'd rather you didn't. I have some things to think over.'

'But Lee. . .' She pouted prettily.

But he didn't stop to argue.

Stacey, her face a picture of frustration, danced on alone for a while before finally coming across to where Mo was clearing the board for a new game.

'Put those damned things away,' she commanded. 'I've got to have a little company or I'll go mad.'

To Jo's surprise, Mo laughed and stood up. 'I guess a little exercise might do me good at that.'

With a cheerful wink at Jo, he left her to pack away the chess pieces and board while he took Stacey into his arms to dance.

Stacey came down later, when Jo was trying

fruitlessly to sleep, but she didn't get into her bunk. She sat in the dim light from the moon, obviously waiting, and when she heard the sounds of Lee coming aboard she went out into the galley.

Her bunk was still empty when Jo woke just after dawn.

So Lee had succumbed after all.

As her mind registered the fact, Jo felt a leaden weight settle in the region of her heart.

They spent the following morning in an exploration of the sea bed around the rocky shoreline of a small island. It was a glorious technicolour underworld almost beyond Jo's imagining. She learned to use the snorkel and mask and was instructed on the more complicated diving equipment—knowledge she was unable to put into practice.

The spare wet suit had a tear in it so she hadn't been able to use it.

'It's too cold down there without a wet suit,' Lee said, his face tight with irritation. He turned to Mo, who was busy strapping his equipment to his back. 'I asked you to make sure every piece of equipment was checked,' Lee told Mo, and it was the first time Jo had heard him use that hard, angry tone to his second-in-command.

'Seems as if I missed that piece. Everyone makes mistakes once in a while.' Mo stood tall and seemed to be issuing a challenge to Lee.

Jo intervened to remind Lee that she would be going back home in less than a week, so it was unlikely she would need a wet suit in the time remaining.

But Lee still seemed angry, more angry than the situation warranted, Jo thought and, for once, Mo's wide grin was absent. The air between the two men almost crackled with tension.

For a moment, Lee seemed about to prolong the argument, but after a brief hesitation he shrugged. 'Dry yourself off and wrap up in a blanket,' he ordered Jo. 'And keep out of the water. The last thing we need right now is for you to catch a chill.'

As he splashed back over the side, Jo heaved a sigh. For a while it had almost seemed as though he was concerned for her welfare. She should have known better.

Stacey flatly refused to have dinner aboard. So now, each evening they went ashore to eat and came back to sit up on the deck for a final nightcap. Mellowed by the good food and drink, Stacey found less difficulty in persuading Lee to dance with her.

They were dancing tonight, the sea behind them, laced with silvery moonlight. The scene was achingly romantic and Jo felt suddenly depressed.

More and more she'd gravitated towards Mo. He'd never met Jocelyn, although he'd obviously heard about her from Lee, so he was able to relate to Jo as herself, which helped bring out the best in her.

She was sitting on the deck with him as Lee and Stacey danced, sipping at a hot chocolate. 'Nothing like a nice cup of cocoa to round off the evening.'

Mo had a Scotch whisky and laughed at her choice of nightcap. 'For Pete's sake, nobody drinks cocoa any more to take them to bed.'

His face seemed flushed, his voice thick and hard around the edges. Jo looked at him and wondered what was bothering him. It surely couldn't have been the few words he'd exchanged with Lee about the wet suit.

He seemed to drink more these days, but perhaps that was because they were going to restaurants to eat, where the wine was unlimited as long as you paid for the food.

'I do,' Jo said, making light of his mood. 'I like it. It doesn't seem to help me sleep the way it used to when I was a child, but I still like it.'

Mo grinned. 'Next time you're having trouble getting to sleep just give me a call.' His hand reached for hers and squeezed it. 'You're not a little girl any more and I have something better than cocoa to send you happy into dreamland.'

His eyes, shining tipsily, held something more than just teasing and there could be no mistaking the invitation he was issuing.

Jo fought down a feeling of disgust. This wasn't the patient, gentle Mo she'd come to know and like so well. 'Mo,' she said, disentangling her hand from his. 'I think you've had a little too much to drink.'

'More than a little, my sweet,' he said, reaching for the whisky bottle to pour some more of the golden liquid into his glass. 'And by the time I've finished, I shall have had more than a lot.'

Jo frowned. She'd begun to feel uneasy and tried

to turn the conversation away from what seemed somehow to be a dangerous moment.

'What's your real name, Mo?'

'Moray,' he said, with a snort. 'Can you imagine any caring parent giving a kid a name like Moray?' He seemed genuinely upset, as though his name had been a lifelong source of resentment.

'I think it's nice,' Jo said firmly. 'Isn't it the name of a place in Scotland?'

'Maybe,' he said. 'But it's also the name of an eel. What do you make of that? They named me after a slippery character like an eel.' He put his arm about Jo's shoulder and brought his lips close to her cheek. 'Now, you don't think I'm an eel, do you, my lovely Jo?'

Jo smelled the whisky heavy on his breath and felt the wet touch of his mouth against her skin. She tried to pull away, but he held her more firmly.

'Come on, honey. Tell me. . .what you think. . . I am. . .'

'A heel, I'd say right now.'

Lee's cool voice cutting through the strangely fraught conversation came like the answer to a prayer, and Jo looked up gratefully.

Reaching down, he took her hand and hauled her to her feet. 'Care to dance?'

'Hey. Can't blame a guy for trying,' Mo said thickly. 'Stop muscling in, man.'

Ignoring Mo's protest, Lee calmly led her to the forward deck and took her into his arms, resting his head against her temple. Jo's body trembled faintly, as much with the shock of Mo's uncharacteristic behaviour as with the fact that she was in Lee's arms.

Over his shoulder, Jo saw Stacey slumped in one of the deep upholstered deck-chairs, a brooding expression on her pretty face.

She shivered and Lee's hand tightened against her spine as they swayed to the slow, romantic rhythm. His breath disturbed tendrils of her hair and now her tremor was all for him.

Jo found herself wondering what magic lay in these arms which seemed to envelop her in a warmth and security that she knew in her heart didn't exist there. Her body curving against the hard line of him felt alive with sensation and she had to fight the urge to wrap her arms about his neck and snuggle closer.

Mo came rather unsteadily across the deck. Involuntarily, Jo flinched and pressed herself more tightly against Lee. But it was Stacey he was heading for.

'I seem to be the best of what's left, honey. Want to dance with me?'

The girl's cool eyes looked upward into Mo's flushed face. 'Get lost,' she said.

CHAPTER EIGHT

Jo was watching Lee from her vantage-point on the harbour wall. He wore denim shorts that reached to just above his knees and was bare from the waist up. She saw the play of taut muscles beneath his tanned skin as he lifted his hands to shade his eyes.

He was standing in the surf of the small crescent beach, studying the water. The sky was bright, but cloudy, the wind fairly brisk, and there were white caps breaking on the ocean some little way out.

Lee was shaking his head as he turned and came walking towards her up the beach. 'Too rough,' he pronounced as he drew nearer. 'I think we'd better stay in harbour today.'

He hauled himself up on to the wall beside her, his arm brushing against her shoulder as he settled himself. It was the nearest he'd come to her since the night Mo had got drunk. He wasn't smiling, but his expression seemed friendly enough and Jo felt her spirits lift a little.

Mo had gone ashore to collect the mail, and Stacey was absent on some business of her own.

'I don't think Stacey will be happy about staying in,' Jo was wryly.

She'd heard the girl complaining to Mo the day before as Lee had ordered the yacht back to harbour as the weather turned brisk.

'What's Lee running here? A kindergarten?' she'd demanded petulantly. 'It seems he's scared that baby will get her feet wet.'

'He's not making that many concessions,' Mo had answered. He'd seemed a little subdued since that night, but his attitude to Jo was just as friendly as it had ever been. 'He is responsible for Jo's safety, since he brought her on board, and sailing can be dangerous.'

'Then why did he bring her?'

Mo had simply shrugged.

The question was a valid one and Jo had frequently wondered the same thing, but, so far, she hadn't been able to find a convincing answer.

'Let me worry about Stacey,' Lee said now.

Back on the *Ilona*, they had a cup of coffee. Lee's eyes seemed to be assessing her from head to foot, as she drank, but he passed no comment.

'You might as well have a day ashore,' he said at last. 'Do some shopping—buy some presents, or whatever. . .'

Jo looked at him, startled. The days seemed to have merged into one another and she seemed to have been here on the yacht for an eternity. With a shock, she realised that it would soon be time to start thinking of going home.

Home! She had difficulty conjuring up a mental picture of the small terraced house where she'd lived all her life. Somehow, the close confines of the yacht had become her whole world. She felt suddenly depressed.

'What is it?' Lee broke into her thoughts, his voice suprisingly gentle. 'Is something bothering you?'

The friendly tone disarmed her and she found herself telling him about her thoughts.

'I know you haven't wanted me here,' she said, 'and it hasn't all been easy, but this holiday is something I'll remember for the rest of my life.' She smiled ruefully into his dark eyes, which had settled quietly on hers. 'When I'm back again sitting in front of my typewriter, I'll remember all the good times.'

'Have there been good times, Jo?'

He sounded almost asthough what she felt mattered, but just talking about it seemed to bring the moment of parting nearer and Jo felt a lump rise in her throat.

'Oh, yes,' she said softly.

He swallowed his coffee and lifted his brows at her. 'Another?'

Jo nodded and he leaned across to pour the hot liquid into her cup, his fingers brushing lightly against her own as he did so. Jo restrained the now familiar tremor.

He settled back into his chair and looked at her. 'So. You'll go back to being a secretary.'

Jo nodded. 'That's if I can find another job. The company I worked for went out of business, making me redundant, and there are a lot of others going the same way. But I dare say I'll find something.'

He nodded slowly. 'You like being a secretary?'

Jo bit her lip. She'd liked it well enough before setting out on this adventure. Now it seemed impossible that she would ever be able to settle back again into the old humdrum days. Now she was a woman in love and she knew it would be a long time before she would be able to forget. . .

But she didn't want him to know that. He thought she had come here, at best, to reclaim him for Jocelyn, and, at worst, to claim him for herself, offering him the outward appearance of his lost love if he was willing to accept.

With an effort, she dredged up a smile. 'It's what I've always done.' She drained her cup and got up.

She couldn't go on sitting here, close to him, his unexpected concern eating through her defences. It was too risky. It would probably end with her spilling out her feelings for him, tempting him into settling for second best. And, if he accepted, she would never forgive him.

'I think I will do some shopping,' she said, though, with her parents dead and Jocelyn gone off goodness knew where, there was no one to buy presents for.

'Right! How d'ya like it?'

Joanne looked up at the reflection of the tall redhead in the mirror and felt the movement of the girl's fingers shaking out the tangles in her hair.

Her visit to the hairdresser had been a spur-of-the-moment thing. She felt nervous and uncertain, but there was something about the girl's cheerful face that put her a little more at ease.

'I was hoping you would be able to suggest something. I'd like to walk out of here looking entirely different.

The redhead had an attractive smile. 'I can't think

why,' she said. 'If I looked half as good as you I'd be one very happy girl.'

Jo flushed. Accepting compliments gracefully had never been easy, but she couldn't deny that the colour in her cheeks, against which her eyes seemed to sparkle a deeper blue, improved the looks she'd always thought of as ordinary. It was strange, but, despite the fact that she shared the same face as her twin, Jocelyn had always seemed to be the beauty.

'Well, I think it might suit you cut shorter, with a drape here.'

Jo shut her eyes. The step before her seemed suddenly enormous. Did she have the courage?

'Just do whatever you like.'

She crossed her fingers in her lap and gave herself up, trying not to wince as the scissors sliced through her thick hair.

'Do you like it?'

The girl gave the last little tweak to the hair at Jo's ears and stood back.

Jo, who had closed her mind and eyes to what was going on, took a wary look at her reflection and confronted a stranger.

'Well, say something.'

After Jo's long, absorbed silence, the girl's voice held a trace of anxiety.

Jo bit her lip, quelling the sense of panic which threatened to overwhelm her. 'It. . .it's wonderful,' she said at last. 'It just doesn't look anything like me.'

'This is you with a new hairstyle, not a portrait,'

the girl said, on a note of relief. 'And I think you look stunning.'

Jo wasn't sure stunning was the word running through Lee's mind as he met up with her at the quayside.

'What in hell have you done to yourself?' he demanded at last.

From his expression it was hard to say if the comment was intended as a complaint or a compliment.

'Don't you like it?'

She felt the colour running hot beneath her skin and could have kicked herself for the anxiety she heard in her voice; the question had been almost a plea.

He scrutinised her for so long, she was on the point of screaming. Then he said, 'You didn't have to do that.'

Jo felt her heart sink. Whatever she had expected him to say, it wasn't this cold, flat statement. And what had he meant? His closed face, so different from the easy friendliness of earlier, made it impossible for her to ask.

Without another word, he stood aside to let her pass.

Jo went below to her shared cabin with a mixture of feelings running riot. She sat down and took another look at her new reflection.

The change in her appearance was startling, even to herself, and her heart beat furiously as she surveyed herself in the tiny mirror. The thick abundance of curls had disappeared. Cut short and sleek against her head, with a thick, eye-catching swathe of hair draped low over her right brow, light tendrils clinging to her cheeks and the nape of her neck, the result was alarming to say the least.

When the hairdresser had removed the cape and towel from her neck with a jaunty flourish, the change had struck her even more forcibly, but after the initial shock had come a peculiar sense of satisfaction. Today, she could be no one but Joanne.

By evening, Mo and Stacey hadn't returned. Jo felt their absence as a relief—somehow the atmosphere seemed easier.

Lee cooked the evening meal. He laid the small folding table up on deck with a starched white cloth and proper cutlery.

In contrast to the earlier days, when there'd been just the three of them and they'd grown into the habit of eating, in the cockpit, long French loaves stuffed with cheeses, salads and meats, or impromptu offerings from whoever felt the urge to cook at the small stove, dinner seemed almost formal.

Lee had prepared chicken, done in a delicious wine sauce with fresh vegetables and a crisp tangy salad. To follow, there were hot pancakes with glazed strawberries and thick cream melting around them.

Without the distraction of Stacey's demanding presence and Mo's moral support, Jo felt strangely marooned.

Alone with Lee for practically the first time since they'd arrived aboard, she felt self-conscious, her nervousness increased by his almost absorbed appraisal of her new look. She'd hardly had time to get used to it herself and wondered what comparisons he was making.

They ate in almost total silence and Jo was relieved when the meal was finally finished. As soon as she decently could, she got up to leave, though there was nowhere to retreat to but her cabin, which was cramped and uncomfortably hot after the heat of the day.

'That was lovely, thank you,' she said formally, standing up. 'Please leave the dishes for me.'

Lee caught her arm. 'I have something I'd like you to see,' he said. 'Come to my cabin.'

Jo shot him a startled glance, searching for the meaning behind the casual command, and he gave her a cynical smile.

'Don't worry—I'm not going to seduce you.'

Jo tried to subdue the tell-tale flush that was rising to her cheeks. 'I didn't think you were,' she lied. But, as she followed him below, her heart beat unsteadily.

He led her into his cabin, ostentatiously leaving the door open wide. Jo hadn't been in here before. A tingle ran the length of her spine as he motioned her to take a seat on the low bed. He reached up to the cupboard above his head, brought out a flat box and handed it to her.

Jo blinked in surprise. Surely he hadn't bought her a present? Whatever she had been expecting, it wasn't this.

'What is it?' she said doubtfully, making no effort to open it.

'You need a wet suit,' he said, taking the box from her and placing it on the bed to open it. He lifted the garment and shook it out. 'I think the size is right, but you'd better try it to make sure.'

Jo suddenly remembered his assessing glances over coffee. He'd been mentally measuring her curves. She flushed. Did he expect her to literally show him how it fitted? 'I'll try it on in my cabin,' she said hurriedly.

He shook his head, an expression of impatience flitting across his face. 'You haven't worn one before—you'll need some help to get into it first time. There's a knack to it.'

Jo's colour deepened. 'If you think. . .'

'Don't be foolish.' He was reaching into the box again. 'If you're worried about protecting your modesty, this should cover it.' He tossed her a turquoise swimsuit and shot her a sardonic look. 'The bathroom's that way.'

Jo locked the bathroom door carefully behind her and heard his mocking laugh. Damn him! She gritted her teeth, wishing there was some way she could shake his cool self-confidence.

His appraisal was anything but cool, as she emerged hesitantly from the bathroom. In the narrow wardrobe mirror, she could see that the swimsuit fitted her curves perfectly, the vibrant colour making her lightly tanned skin look like honeyed silk. With her new hairstyle, she looked positively glamorous.

A low whistle issued from his pursed lips. 'That's really something,' he said softly.

Jo, squirming under his close scrutiny, nevertheless felt a thrill of satisfaction. For once, he was looking at her as herself—not as a reflection of her sister.

'Do you think we could get on with it?' she said coldly.

He shrugged. 'OK. Let's go!'

If his scrutiny was embarrassing, the help he gave her in getting into the wet suit was excruciating. His hands gripped and tugged and smoothed with ruthlessly calm precision. Jo's pulse rose rapidly and her skin burned where it made contact with his hand. And her discomfort was all the more acute because, from his set expression, the contact left him completely unmoved.

'Get it to fit properly here,' he instructed, smoothing his hand upwards from her thigh to her waist and across the small of her back to the other side. His head was bent close to her shoulder, and she could smell his fresh, tangy aftershave and feel the electric warmth of him. To her horror, Jo found herself struggling with a terrible urge to put her cheek against his, to brush her lips against the corner of his mouth. She pulled back sharply.

He lifted his head immediately and gave her an enquiring look. 'Problems?' He raised dark brows. 'Does anything hurt?'

Jo swallowed down her sense of panic and licked her dry lips. 'No. No. Everything's fine. Very comfortable, so far.'

Nothing hurts, she thought, with a surge of bitterness, as much as having to pretend I don't want you like mad every time you come near me. I'm a lost cause. . .and I hate it.

She heaved a sigh of relief when the garment had finally been fitted to his satisfaction.

'Seems OK,' he said at last, running his hand down the curve of her back in a gesture of finality. 'Does it feel OK?'

'Lovely.' Jo could hear the ragged sound of her own breathing. 'If you don't mind, I'll just go and have a look in the bathroom mirror.'

The look he gave her was wry, full of apparent understanding, which had her colour flaring along with her temper.

It was a relief to shut the bathroom door behind her. She leaned, with her back against it, until her heart stopped banging and her breathing returned to normal. If having him help to put the suit on affected her this much, there was no way she could risk letting him take it off again.

Minutes later, when her self-control seemed to have returned, she peeled the wet suit off and then the swimsuit and dressed herself, running her fingers through her ruffled hair and pressing cool hands against her flaming cheeks.

'Are you going to be in there all night?' Lee's irritable growl reached her through the door and she opened it hastily.

He looked at her for a long moment before a slow smile spread across his tanned face.

'Spoilsport,' was all he said, and Jo knew he had

observed and understood every emotion that had passed through her treacherous body.

'If you've finished with me, I'd like to go to bed,' she said, furious that her colour was rising again. 'Since you've got me the wet suit, I assume we'll be sailing early tomorrow.'

He nodded, the amused smile still hovering maddeningly about his lips. 'Uh-huh! I agree it would seem obvious.'

They were three or four miles from shore when Jo saw the dark shape break the surface of the sea. Her first reaction was fear. It looked like some huge dark sea monster. Then she saw the large head lifting clear and the spouting burst of water.

'Whale!' she yelled, with sudden excitement. 'Whale to starboard!'

There were two of them. Jo watched in silent fascination as they moved alongside with slow, easy movements, which nevertheless kept pace with the boat. As she peered over the rail, other grey shapes became discernible.

'Well spotted.' Lee was alongside her, a pleased smile on his dark face. 'Cut the engine, Mo. There's half a dozen of them and they're cruising.'

'Isn't it wonderful?' Unthinkingly, Jo grasped Lee's arm and held on tightly. 'I didn't think they'd come so close.'

For a moment, Lee's fingers covered her hand, squeezing in sympathetic understanding of her wonder. She almost gasped with shock at his unexpected friendliness.

Stacey came and stood alongside Lee. 'About time we saw some action.'

'They're stopping.' Mo joined them. 'Maybe we'll get a chance to go in with them—take some film.'

Jo's stomach contracted as she remembered her adventure with the dolphins, but these creatures were much larger and, in her mind, far more menacing.

'But isn't it dangerous?' she asked cautiously.

Mo grinned. 'Sure.'

'Only if you get too near,' Lee cut in. 'Get the wet suits. They're not going to hang about all day.'

Mo disappeared below, reappearing quickly with wet suits over his arm. Stacey was already smoothing a colourful suit, supple as a second skin, over her shapely body, her face aglow with anticipation. She shot a look at Jo that dared her to follow her lead, the cynical twist of her lips proclaiming her certainty that Jo didn't have the courage.

And, if Jo was honest, she would have had to admit that her insides were quaking like aspen leaves in a breeze. And yet, perversely, she knew it was an experience she couldn't let go. How much the feeling had to do with Stacey's unspoken challenge she couldn't say, but it was as much for her own satisfaction.

'Mo, would you mind helping me with my wet suit?'

She caught Lee's quick glance, saw the cynical amusement there and something else, dark and glittering, which made her catch her breath. 'Stacey can do that,' he said abruptly. 'Mo, is that camera loaded?'

Stacey's face set mutinously. 'I've got better things to do than play wet-nurse.'

Lee's brows lowered. 'Never mind the jokes, just do it.'

He didn't hang around long enough to discover that Stacey wasn't joking.

'You are a pain in the ass, lady,' she said contemptuously to Jo, as the men splashed overboard. 'Why don't you just shove off where you belong?'

The pure venom which shot from Stacey's eyes into her own before the girl went over the side to join the men had Jo shaking more than her fear of going in with the whales. It was a tremor compounded partly of frustrated anger and partly a sense of hopelessness. With the exception of Mo, she thought, she'd do better to live among hostile Indians.

After only a moment's hesitation, she went below to fetch the wet suit Lee had given her. As she took it from its box, she had consciously to suppress the memories it aroused, of Lee's hands against her and her own insane longings to turn his workmanlike stroking into caresses.

She wondered, with some judicious malice, how Stacey would have reacted had she asked Lee to help her on with the wet suit and he had complied, performing the same sensual ritual as before, his hands missing no part of her as they swept across her breasts and down into the private hollow between her thighs. . .

With a gasp, Jo caught herself up. What on earth was her mind playing at? Wasn't it bad enough having to endure what she had to, without foisting upon her the pain of its own senseless fantasies?

But somehow she'd learned well the intricacies of getting into the wet suit and it wasn't long before she was lowering herself gingerly into the water wearing a snorkel and mask rather than the more complicated breathing apparatus.

Beneath the surface, it was like an enchanted world. The sun slanted through, shimmering pale green to darkest aquamarine. The huge creatures seemed almost stationary, suspended effortlessly with only the slightest movement of their giant tails. Lee and Mo moved slowly about them, angling the camera, while just above their heads Stacey swam gracefully, as though performing in some underwater ballet.

She turned suddenly and saw Jo, who was drawing tentatively near. Her eyes spat fire, even in this environment. With a gesture reminiscent of an animal guarding its territory against an intruder, she moved possessively closer to the whales.

Jo was suddenly short of breath. Turning upward, she broke the surface and blew through the snorkel, stopping a second or two to breathe fresh air, before taking a deep breath for the plunge.

Submerged once more, she saw that Stacey was within arm's length of the smaller of the whales. Mo had the camera trained on her and she was obviously loving it. Jo swam slowly nearer, edging warily to the rear of the animal. Its huge eye was somehow intimidating. The creature's underside was encrusted with what Jo supposed were barnacles, and she wondered inanely if they made the poor thing feel uncomfortable.

She was almost level with the huge tail when it began to swing towards her. Unlike its former somnolent sway, the movement was like the lash of a whip and Jo felt the pressure of the water it displaced before she understood the portent.

Suddenly, she was seized from behind, a hand on her head pushing her violently down and away. Involuntarily, she gasped and swallowed water and her hand went up in an automatic and frenzied effort to tear the clamp from her nose so she could breathe. But the hands were there again, propelling her strongly upwards until her head burst through the surface of the water. The mask and snorkel were torn from her and Lee's face, contorted with some emotion that seemed a mixture of fear and fury, glared into hers.

But there was little time to react as she sucked in air and the painful, racking coughing began.

He turned her expertly in the water so that she lay on her back and hooked an arm about her from the rear, clasping her against him as he began to swim back towards the yacht.

Jo relaxed gratefuly against him and gradually her lungs cleared and the coughing stopped.

As they reached the side, he shoved her, none too gently, up the rope-ladder, and Jo thought with insane inanity that all of her sojourns into the underwater world seemed to end in the same way, with herself collapsed on the deck and a furious Lee towering above her. But, this time, the fury seemed not to be directed against her. To her amazement, he discarded his breathing equipment quickly on to the boards and hauled her up, clasping her tightly against him.

'You little fool,' he rasped. 'You almost got yourself killed.'

Jo's protests that she had done nothing she could think of as wrong were smothered by the sudden fierce pressure of his mouth against hers. The kiss lasted only a second or two and was more painful than pleasurable, but shook her to the soles of her feet, accompanied as it was by a terrible haggard expression made worse by the yellowed tinge of his bronzed face.

Just as suddenly, he released her and turned around. Stacey was coming aboard close behind Mo and he turned his ravaged face to her.

'Well, Miss Exhibitionist,' he stormed, 'I hope you're pleased with yourself.'

Stacey's colour turned a deep, dull red. 'It wasn't my fault,' she retaliated. 'I didn't know the idiot would go down towards the tail. Anyone with an ounce of brains would know that was the end to avoid.'

Lee took a step towards her, his fists clenched into tight balls of fury. 'If I thought for one moment you touched that fin on purpose, I'd. . .'

Stacey retreated before the murderous intent in his eyes and Mo stepped in between and grasped Lee's arms.

'Hey, hey, Lee!' he said soothingly. 'We had a near accident on our hands just then.' He released a hand to cross himself with superstitious piety. 'Thank heaven that's all it was.'

His large frame blotted Stacey from Lee's vision, and Lee paused, shaking his head like a dog ridding himself of an annoying fly. Jo watched the swift rise and fall of his chest beginning to subside and her own heartbeat slowed against her aching rib-cage.

'Yeah,' Lee said, with another swift shake of his head. 'I guess I got carried away.'

Mo sighed and released his hold. 'Yeah,' he agreed. 'I kind of panicked myself there for a while. It's no surprise.'

Stacey stepped out from behind Mo, her face thunderous now that the danger of violence had obviously passed. 'You surely don't think I'm a mind-reader,' she said belligerently. 'In any case, I'd have to be a pretty special kind to read the mind of a whale and know what it was going to do with its damned tail.'

Lee's colour had returned and he seemed consciously to relax the tight clench of his fists. 'You're experienced enough to know whales don't like being touched.' His voice was steely, his dark eyes chips of ice. 'Any time you feel like showing off again, make sure there's no one else around to bear the brunt.'

Stacey visibly relaxed and her lips drew together in a pout. 'Come on, Lee. Can't you allow a girl one little mistake?'

Lee nodded, a thin smile curving his lips. 'One,

maybe, but not two. That's something you should remember.' He turned suddenly to Jo. 'You've just learned a valuable lesson,' he said harshly. 'Let's hope you take heed.' To Mo, he said, 'Turn her around. We're going back into harbour.'

CHAPTER NINE

IT WAS warm and the cabin seemed even more claustrophobic than usual.

The bunk opposite was empty again, as it was most nights, and Jo felt the dark thrust of pain. A mental picture of Stacey making love with Lee rose in her mind's eye to taunt her and she felt sick with jealousy.

What a hypocrite he was. In the day he treated Stacey as though she were nothing but a member of the crew and more often than not he seemed to be angry with her, but at night she crept to meet him, stealing back just after dawn.

Jo's throat was dry and she thought longingly of a cup of tea. She felt reluctant to get up and go out into the galley in case she disturbed the lovers and brought herself face to face with the evidence of the truth of all her surmising.

Anger burned through her. Why should she lie here, parched for a drink, afraid she would discover what she already knew existed?

She got out of bed and went through into the small galley. She rattled a cup into its saucer and was tempted to bang the kettle on to the stove, but thought better of it. Her emotions were strangely volatile and she wasn't at all sure that, in this mood, she would be able to control her temper.

It's none of your business, she reminded herself forcefully. Lee was adult, a free agent and he could please himself who he slept with. Why then did he bother to hide it? And why did she feel betrayed?

She made the tea strong and sweet, feeling she needed that more than the medium and sugarless brew she normally drank. She carried it up on deck.

The sea was dark, riffled by a light breeze. She took a deep breath, feeling the cool air calming her nerves, easing the tension, and moved slowly towards the forward deck, where she leaned on the rail, taking slow appreciative sips at her tea.

As her eyes travelled lazily over the shadowy deck, she became aware that someone had brought a mattress up to sleep on deck and was suddenly reminded of what Lee had told her. That, on warm nights, he sometimes slept bare up here. She could see the movement of a bulky shape beneath a blanket, as the moon reflected palely off the sea, and couldn't repress a guilty thrill at the thought of him naked and so near.

The shape moved again and she heard a man's throaty murmur followed by the low sound of a woman's answering cry.

Realisation dawned of what she was watching even before the blanket slipped to reveal the out-flung female arm, and the moon glinted on the pale gold of blonde hair that shrouded the face of the man. How could she have forgotten the significance of Stacey's empty bunk?

Cup and saucer fell from her nerveless fingers and Jo just left them where they fell in her haste to get away. As she stumbled below, her foot slipping on the bottom step, hands caught her about the waist. With a gasp, she turned and stared into Lee's face and for a moment the world swam dizzily.

He supported her for a moment, before putting her back on her feet. His eyes narrowed coldly on her startled face.

'I heard the cups rattle and thought Mo was making coffee,' he said, adding disdainfully, 'If you and he wanted to remain undisturbed, you should have taken greater care. Especially after your demonstration of modesty.'

His hand ran lightly up her bare arm, sliding under the flimsy cotton at the shoulder. Her skin responded by bursting into flame, but as she made to move away from him his fingers gripped her upper arms.

'Hardly discreet to be wandering about half naked. Entrancing though the sight might be, it makes assumptions very easy.'

Jo's temper suddenly asserted itself. 'Making assumptions seems to be your favourite pastime. It doesn't seem to occur to you that you might be wrong.'

He gave a short laugh. 'No. That doesn't occur to me often, I agree.' His eyes held hers mercilessly. 'In this case, it should be pretty easy to find out whether I'm right or wrong.'

He released her arms and moved towards the steps, where he stopped and indicated with mock courtesy that she should precede him. 'Would you like to lead the way?'

She stared at him helplessly, her brain whirling with a mixture of emotions. Outrage that Lee thought it was she who had been lying with Mo in his makeshift bed and some confused desire to stop Lee finding out it was Stacey, though who she was trying to protect in the latter instance it was impossible to say. She just knew she couldn't let him go up and find Stacey naked in Mo's arms.

'I don't have to lead you anywhere,' she said, as outrage gained the upper hand. 'If you want to make a fool of yourself, you can do it alone. I'm going back to bed.'

Face burning, she fled to her bunk.

Stacey was back in her bunk and sleeping soundly when Jo got back to the cabin. Jo stared in amazement, her mind doubting, for a moment, the reality of what she'd thought had happened on deck. Common sense told her it hadn't been a dream, and that Stacey must have found another way back to the cabin which didn't entail going through the kitchen.

Jo's stomach tightened in dismay. If Lee really did go up on deck to check whether Mo was there, he would find him alone. And make one of his 'easy' assumptions. Unless Mo too had gone back to his cabin. Over and over Jo told herself she didn't care what Lee thought about her, but it was a long time before she went to sleep.

Mo was in the kitchen before Jo the following morning, making a note of provisions they'd need to pick up on the morning's shopping expedition. They shopped by rote in twos, Lee and Stacey one day and Jo with Mo the next.

He gave her a sheepish grin as she reached around him for the kettle. 'Sorry about the shock. But a guy like me's got to take love where it's offered.'

'I wouldn't call that love,' she said, evading his eyes and shrinking away from the hand he tried to place on her shoulder. 'But it's not my business, Mo.'

It was silly, but she felt let down. Added to that, of course, she had no way of knowing what had happened after she'd gone to bed last night. . .what Lee might have seen, and what conclusions he might have reached. It's none of his damned business anyway, she told herself in silent fury, but her hand shook as she poured herself a cup of coffee.

Lee came in as she was pouring herself a second cup. 'I'll have coffee, if there's one going.'

Jo nodded, unable to meet his eyes. 'Do you want toast?'

'No, thanks.'

His tone told her nothing, but she didn't dare risk a glance at his face.

He took the list from Mo's hand. 'I'll do the shopping this morning. You can take the rota with Stacey tomorrow.'

'OK.'

Mo seemed unabashed. If Lee hadn't gone up on deck last night after all, then it was likely his easy grin sprang from blissful ignorance.

'You'll come wih me,' Lee told Jo as he took the

coffee she handed him. 'Make it snappy. I'll be on deck when you're ready.'

She tried to gauge his mood as he strode alongside her in the shopping centre, but his face was remote, his expression inscrutable.

It wasn't until they'd completed the shopping and stopped for a breather and a cup of coffee at a pavement café that she felt the urge to try and straighten things out. Perhaps she should have told him the truth immediately last night, or encouraged him to go up and find out for himself before Stacey had had the chance to steal quietly away.

As she sipped her coffee uncertainly, it came to her with sudden insight that she had been protecting Lee, not Mo. After Jocelyn's desertion of him, she hadn't wanted him to find out that Stacey was also betraying him with another man. Which was ridiculous, Jo told herself scathingly, because he obviously didn't care a damn about her own feelings.

But she still found herself wanting to put things right between them on that score. She wouldn't have to implicate Stacey. Just confess to him that she might have misled him about the kind of friendship she had with Mo and deny she had slept with him last night.

'Lee,' she began hesitantly, 'this probably isn't the right moment. . .'

He stopped sipping his coffee and looked into her troubled face. 'You're right,' he said. 'This isn't the right moment.'

Surprisingly, his hand briefly covered her fingers as they drummed nervously on the table. He took his hand away almost immediately, but his touch burned against her skin for a long time afterwards.

On the way back to harbour, a tall, darkly tanned man gripped Lee's arm, pulling him to a halt.

'Why, Lee! Talk of the devil, and here he is!'

Lee's face broke into a broad smile. 'Frank! As one devil to another, how are you?'

'Fine.' Frank gripped Lee's hand with obvious pleasure. 'How about you? Still making the millions?'

'Sure.' Lee nodded. 'Somebody's got to now you've defected to the easy life.'

Frank laughed. 'Best thing I ever did—selling out my business to retire down here. Found out there's more to life than cultivating money and ulcers. Nowadays I've got time to pay some attention to my wife. You remember Marie.' He was holding the hand of a petite brunette and pulled her forward. She had a quiet face and a lovely smile.

'Sure I do.' Lee kissed her. 'How are you doing, Marie?'

'I'm fine.' The little woman eyed Jo with friendly curiosity. 'I heard you'd got yourself an English fiancée,' she said.

Jo's smile froze and her eyes rose apprehensively to Lee, but apart from a slight stiffening of his body he seemed unperturbed.

'That's right. I did.'

Jo waited, wondering how he would choose to tell his friends his engagement was over, but he remained silent.

Frank's brown eyes swept Jo appreciatively. 'And a real beauty at that. . .you lucky guy.'

Jo coloured, embarrassed by the compliment and the fact that Frank obviously thought she was Jocelyn.

She saw Lee smile, a wry lifting of the corners of his mouth, and thought it boded ill. Frank couldn't know he'd touched on a raw nerve.

Lee inhaled on a sigh. 'Oh, yeah! I seem to get all the luck where women are concerned.'

Jo bit her lip. He was thinking of Cyndi, of Jocelyn and now he believed that she too was having an affair with Mo right under his nose.

But he had no feelings for her, so why should it bother him, even if it had been true? His pride, she guessed. For once it seemed as though Mo had got the girl, and it hurt, even though, dog in the manger, he didn't want that particular girl himself.

'Marie and I are celebrating our tenth anniversary tonight with a party,' Frank was saying. 'Why don't you bring the little lady along about eight-thirty?'

Jo thought Lee would refuse, but to her surprise he nodded.

'Sounds good,' he said, and hooked a casual arm about Jo's shoulders. 'What do you say, Jo?'

Startled, Jo could only nod.

'Fine. Fine.' Frank beamed.

The two men shook hands.

'Who else is on board with you?'

'Mo Delaney and Stacey Trent.'

'Fine,' Frank said again, his beam widening. 'Bring them along too.'

'Thanks,' Lee said. 'See you about eight-thirty.'

Stacey was excited when Lee casually dropped the news of the party invitation as they sat in the cockpit drinking coffee.

'Well, thank goodness for some excitement at last,' she said, her eyes glowing. 'Frank Curtin, huh! And still married to that little shadow of his. I must say I didn't expect it to last this long. A couple of years ago, it seemed. . .'

Stacey stopped suddenly, realising that there were ears listening to her reminiscences.

'That so?' Lee laughed softly, but his eyes held a glint of something Jo thought looked like anger. 'You knew Frank before he—er—retired, did you, Stacey?'

Stacey seemed reluctant to meet his searching eyes. 'Sure. I crewed for him some years ago.'

Lee nodded agreeably. 'Well, tonight you'll have the opportunity to remake his acquaintance. I'm sure Frank will be delighted.'

Jo suddenly had a strong hunch that Lee knew it was Stacey who'd slept up on deck with Mo, and wondered what was going through his mind. At the moment, it really must seem to him that every woman in his world found it impossible to be faithful.

Stacey, for once, seemed impervious to the atmosphere and couldn't hide her excitement. Jo was in the cabin as the girl tried on one dress after another.

'There's more than five hours to go before the party tonight, Stacey. Aren't you getting yourself a little wound up?'

'Sure. And if you've ever been to one of these parties, you'd be wound up too. The people who will be there are the kind who just never have to worry about money. They'll just freeze you out cold if you don't look the part. And I've got absolutely nothing to wear.'

Jo laughed wryly. 'Well, if you haven't, I'm sure I haven't. But people will just have to take me as I am.'

'Then they just won't take you, lady,' Stacey told her with a haughty toss of her blonde head. 'Where's Lee?'

'Up on deck reading.'

He certainly wasn't excited about the party, Jo noticed ruefully. Since they'd come back with the shopping, he'd been in a brown study, his dark brows drawn low on his forehead.

He was frowning up at Stacey as Jo joined them on deck.

'I just haven't anything I wouldn't be ashamed to be seen wearing in your company,' she was complaining. 'Back home, I could probably pick up something reasonable for the money I could afford, but the boutiques here are *so* expensive.'

Lee's mouth drew down at the corners. 'Everything, everywhere's expensive when people think you have money,' he said cynically. 'Get what you need and charge it to my account.'

'Oh, Lee! Thanks a million.'

Stacey flew at him in delight, raining kisses on his face, acting for all she was worth as though she had no idea he would respond to her complaints with such generosity.

'I hope it's not going to cost me a million,' he said drily, pushing her away with a touch of irritation as she continued to show her gratitude with kisses. 'You'd better go before the best is gone. My guess is the boutiques will be doing big business out of this party tonight.'

'Oh, lord! Yes!'

Jo watched as Stacey went scuttling off, her expression a mixture of anxiety and determination, which said plainly that no one but she was going to get the best if she could help it.

'You'd better go with her,' Lee said casually.

Jo looked at him with a frown. 'Why should I do that?'

I should think that's obvious.'

The frown vanished and anger took its place. 'You mean. . .to get myself a dress. . .and charge it to your account?'

He answered her fury with calm. 'You want to look good, don't you?'

'Ah! So I have to dress to impress people I don't know and who don't know me, and who I'll never see again once I get back home,' she said sarcastically. 'And, to do that, I have to take money from you.' She nodded tightly. 'Oh, I can see how you'd like that—to put me in the same category as Stacey and keep me there.'

A low growl sounded in his throat. 'You can see nothing beyond that stubborn English nose of yours.' He leapt violently to his feet and gripped her arms, and Jo thought wildly that he would soon be wearing grooves in her flesh from his fingers. 'And even Stacey has it right this time. In my company, a woman is expected to have the best—to look the best.'

Jo's mouth flew open in disbelief. 'Why, you. . . conceited——'

'Not conceited,' he cut coldly across her heated words. 'Just realistic. I can't change what is.'

'No?' Jo retaliated, struggling to release herself from him. 'But do you have to condone it—perpetuate it—this self-agrandising snobbery?'

She pulled away harder and he let go of her so suddenly that she staggered back, her face flushed with fury, her breast rising with every short, irregular breath.

'I'll go as I am,' she said in a hoarse voice. 'And if you don't want to be seen in my company. . .that suits me fine.'

'Well. This is some party,' Mo said, his eyes circling the room with its bevy of beautiful, and not so beautiful people.

Stacey had been right, Joe thought ruefully. Everyone, male and female, was dressed to kill. Only she and Mo stood out, to her mind, like a pair of sore thumbs.

He wore a shirt which strained across his broad chest and a tie which seemed about to choke him and Jo couldn't help but feel proud of him among this group of tailor's window dummies.

She'd ransacked her small wardrobe for the simplest dress she could find, a straight, slim primrose-yellow linen, which dipped demurely in a V to the soft rise of her breasts, edged in pale and delicate lace. It made her look young and vulnerable, which was precisely how she felt standing just inside the doorway of the large, elegant, flower-decked room.

'Perhaps we should have brought a present,' she muttered to Mo as she spied the long table groaning under a mass of elaborately wrapped parcels.

'Among that lot, honey, it would never be noticed.'

Jo laughed. 'I'm sure you're right.'

To her embarrassment, Jo didn't go unnoticed. She felt the eyes which appraised her; the women probably to compare the richness of their attire with the simplicity of hers and smile contemptuous smiles; the men probably because they thought she was the hired help and wondered what she was doing with a glass in her hand.

Lee had gone in ahead of them in his immaculate suit and was circulating among the guests, most of whom seemed to know him well.

Jo had refused to enter the room with him and he hadn't tried to persuade her. She'd regretted her childishness almost at once as she went in behind him alone and unsure of herself, until Mo's large hand had slipped through the crook of her elbow.

One glance at his idea of the right kind of gear for this party and she felt relaxed and almost happy.

'Mo Delaney!' someone called, and Mo turned to

grip the outstretched hand of a short man with a large nose and a curved Spanish moustache.

'Cy!' he said. 'How have you been?'

'Not bad, not bad.'

'Cy Harding,' Mo said to Jo. 'The guy who almost got me into pictures.'

'Not for want of trying, boy. Not for want of trying.'

It seemed necessary for him to say everything twice, Jo noticed, hiding a smile.

'Aren't you going to introduce me?' Cy eyed Jo up and down in a frank assessment which brought the colour to her cheeks.

'This is Joanne Sutton,' Mo said. 'She's out from England and crewing for us.' He looked at Jo's face and laughed. 'Don't worry. He looks at all women like that, with the cash register he calls a brain reckoning up the dollars.'

Jo looked at him, perplexed, and he laughed again.

'Don't let it bother you.'

Cy took her hand and tried to draw her to his side. 'I'd really like to talk to you, sweetie.'

He was good-looking in a rough sort of way, beautifully dressed and his hands dripped with gold.

Jo felt herself recoil.

Mo pushed him away. 'Later, Cy. Later.'

He gripped Jo's arm and began to steer her among the crowd, his head way above most of the others and craning towards the bar.

'Let's get another drink.'

CHAPTER TEN

EVEN in her light dress, Jo felt the heat like a warm enveloping blanket. It brought a film of perspiration out on her forehead and a strong desire for some fresh air. The room reeked with perfume, the combined scents of flowers and every woman in the room. It was suddenly overpowering.

Slowly, she edged around the room, making for the nearest exit.

Mo had left her twenty minutes earlier for what must have been his tenth drink. She could see him now in the corner nearest the bar, looking a little the worse for wear, his tie askew and his hair unruly. His chin was on his chest and he was staring moodily ahead at Stacey, who was dancing with Frank.

He was holding her so close that they seemed to be melded together, and Jo wondered what his nice little wife, Marie, might be thinking about that on this night of their anniversary.

Lee was nowhere to be seen.

Jo felt a hand on her arm and stifled a sigh as she recognised Cy Harding.

'Hello, hello,' he said, gripping her elbow firmly. 'How about you and me having that little chat now, hey. . .how about it?'

'I was just going outside to the garden,' Jo said as he steered her towards a vacant corner, but she might have saved her breath, because Cy wasn't listening.

'Sutton,' he said. 'Yeah! Sure! I thought the name sounded familiar. . .real familiar. And you're doing pretty big in the modelling world at the moment, isn't that so?'

'I'm sorry,' Jo broke in. 'But you've got the wrong girl——'

'Have you thought about changing your agent?' Cy asked, adding confidentially, 'Whatever you're making right now I could treble it for you. I mean treble it. What d'ya say?'

'Well, that would be lovely, but I'm not Jocelyn Sutton,' Jo cut in a little desperately. 'She's my sister—my twin.'

Cy had already started another sentence when her words finally penetrated. 'Whatever percentage you're paying. . .' His mouth stayed open for a second, then he said, 'You're kidding.'

'No. No, I'm not.' Jo was glad to have made contact at last. 'I'm not a model—and I wouldn't know how to be.'

He chewed his lip silently for a moment, his eyes flicking over Jo with that same assessing look she'd suffered earlier.

'Yeah. I thought you looked different—changed your image, so to speak—but no. . .' He nodded slowly. 'I can see now. The same girl. . .but with something extra. . .a kind of class—you could be even bigger in the model world than your sister. . .'

Jo felt her colour rising as he continued to scrutinise her. His voice was loud and it seemed as though other people were beginning to take an interest.

'If you don't mind. . .it's hot, and I'd like to go out into the garden.'

'Sure. Sure.' He was digging into his inside pocket and brought out a small square of pasteboard. 'My card.'

To her astonished annoyance, he pushed it into the neckline of her dress, tucking it expertly beneath the straps of her bra.

'Come and see me tomorrow,' he said, with a little pat of his hand against her cheek. 'I can do a lot for you, sweetie—I mean a lot—believe me. . .'

Jo made her escape at last, reaching the tall windows which led out on to a terrace. As she stepped out into the star-filled night, she cast an anxious glance over her shoulder, sighing with relief to see that he hadn't followed her.

The moon was clear and a thin breeze blew in off the sea making her shiver a little. But it was good to be outside and she took a long, deep breath of the cool air.

The garden was discreetly lit, with low lanterns in the small arbours and coloured lights strung out in the trees, but Jo soon found it was too embarrassing to walk alone along its stone paths. Every nook and cranny seemed to be inhabited by amorous couples. She turned and made her way back towards the house.

On the terrace, she found a secluded corner and then groaned to see the dark outline of a man and a cigar glowing in the dim light.

Cy Harding was her first thought and she turned hurriedly away.

'So you came to find me,' Lee said. 'I hoped you might.'

Jo stopped and turned back and now she could make out his face, a sardonic smile curving his sensuous lips.

'Did you?' Jo sighed with relief and sat down beside him. He was obviously in a tormenting mood, but even so he was a welcome sight after the past few moments with Cy Harding. 'Now why should I do that?'

'Because you can't resist me,' he said.

Jo's stomach clenched. He was teasing, of course, but she hoped he didn't realise how close he'd come to the truth.

'I felt like a breath of fresh air,' she said, deciding the safest way of dealing with his provocative banter was to ignore it.

'You *look* like a breath of fresh air,' he said unexpectedly, startling her into a laugh.

'You mean like a milkmaid among the aristocracy?' she sighed. 'You were right about my outfit. I just don't fit in.'

'No,' he agreed. 'You don't.'

Jo gasped and then laughed again. 'You were meant to argue with me, reassure me I was wrong.'

He shook his head slowly, his eyes appraising her. 'You're not wrong. You fit in here about as much as a fresh wild rose would fit into a display of cultivated orchids.'

Jo stared at him, searching for the mocking light in his eyes, but his face was sober.

She turned away, unable to think of an answer to

give him, unsure of where the conversation was leading. She thought it best to change the subject.

'Gosh, it's hot in there.'

'Yeah.' He seemed happy to follow her lead.

He sat back and inhaled the aromatic smoke from his cigar. Jo remembered Mo telling her he always smoked when he was worried. She wondered if he'd seen Stacey in Frank's arms and come out here to cool his temper? Poor man. He really wasn't having too good a day.

He took the cigar from his mouth and studied the burning tip. 'Are you out here waiting for Mo?' he asked suddenly.

Jo's head turned in surprise. 'No. Of course not. Why should I be?' Then, as the penny dropped, she opened her mouth and breathed out a sigh. 'Ah! I see.' Now was obviously the time to tell him the truth about last night. 'Look, Lee! I have to get something straight with you. I wasn't up on deck with Mo last night.'

He nodded. 'I know. It was Stacey.'

Jo bit her lip and lowered her head. 'Yes, it was. I'm sorry, Lee.'

There was a pause in which she dared not look at him and then he moved towards her, hooking a finger beneath her chin so that she was forced to meet his gaze.

'Sorry? About what?'

She felt the colour rushing into her face and wished she could turn away from his intent, searching eyes. 'I think you know what I mean,' she said

at last. 'It must have been a shock to find out Stacey
was sleeping with Mo as well as with you.'

He tossed his cigar away without taking his eyes
from her face. 'Might I ask what led you to believe
I'm sleeping with Stacey?' he asked steadily.

Jo's face burned more fiercely. 'We share a cabin,'
she said irritably. 'When her bunk is empty every
night. . . Did you expect me not to notice?'

'Oh!' he said quietly, an odd expression lighting
his features. 'And so you thought I'd be upset to
find her on deck with Mo?'

Jo nodded mutely.

'And what about you? Weren't you upset for
yourself?'

'Me?' Jo echoed in surprise and then paused to
recall and try to analyse her feelings of the night
before.

'In a way, I suppose so. I was angry at your
assumption that, just because I was friendly with
Mo, I was automatically sleeping with him. But also,
I didn't want you to go up there. . .and find. . .'

She stopped suddenly, realising that, with every
word, she was giving herself away.

He cupped her face in his hands. 'You weren't
upset for yourself, but only for me?' he queried
softly.

Jo felt a tremor deep inside. His hands were so
gentle, so tender, as though. . . She felt sudden
unexpected tears welling in her eyes.

'After Cyndi,' she whispered. 'And then
Jocelyn. . .I thought. . .'

She felt him stiffen. 'Cyndi? How come you know about Cyndi?'

Jo caught her bottom lip between her teeth, wishing suddenly she'd kept her mouth shut. 'I wormed the story out of Mo,' she admitted in a small voice. 'He didn't want to tell me.'

'I bet he didn't,' Lee said grimly. 'Then how come you knew there was a story to tell?'

'There had to be,' Jo said urgently. 'I just couldn't understand the way your mind worked with regard to women. . .to me. You couldn't accept my reason for coming out here and there had to be some story behind your bitter refusal to trust me. . . I mean— that is—apart from the one experience with. . .my sister. . .'

He smiled a cold smile. 'Oh, yes, there's a story all right. Perhaps more stories than I care to remember—of greed and deceit. . . And your. . .sister was no different.' His mouth twisted ironically at one corner. 'What reason do I have to assume you are?'

Her eyes were lifted to his, indignation making them glisten in the pale moonlight. 'Because I've told you the truth. I don't want anything from you.'

The probing dark eyes seemed to scorch into her mind, into her heart. 'Are you sure of that?' he said softly.

'Very sure.'

His finger touched against her face, explored the contours of her cheek, sending strange, painful shafts of sensation through her.

'Oh, lord!' he said, his voice suddenly ragged. 'You're either a wonderful actress, or. . .'

He broke off and roughly gathered her against him, his lips descending hungrily on hers.

His kiss was agony, arousing a longing so instantaneous and strong that she knew she wasn't going to be able to fight him if it went on.

His kiss deepened and he began to caress her, his fingers brushing the smooth skin of her throat, tracing the neckline of her dress; his hand, sliding over her breasts and down to clasp her waist, gave a tantalising promise which had her shivering.

Oh, lord! she cried silently. If only this was for me. If only I dared believe. . .

Instinctively, she arched closer to him. Her hands, creeping up about his neck, felt the shock of contact with his skin, the texture of his hair, and a whimper of need broke from her lips.

He lifted his head at the sound and looked deep into her dilated eyes. 'Are you still sure there's nothing you want from me?' he asked with gentle mockery.

She stared back at him, mesmerised by the exciting gleam in his dark eyes, by the expression on his face which told her clearly what he wanted from her. He dipped his head to kiss her forehead, her eyes, which had closed in submission, the tip of her nose, the corners of her mouth.

'Jo.' He said her name softly and her heart swelled with emotion. Was it possible he really had forgotten the past. 'My little wild English rose.'

'Oh, Lee!' she whispered, thrilled just to be saying his name.

His hand caressed her back, her waist, moving

inexorably up to her breast, cupping her gently and then exploringly. As her bones seemed about to melt, he paused and moved back a little. She gasped as he put his hand deliberately inside the neckline of her dress and withdrew something.

'What the hell. . .?'

Jo laughed uncomfortably, all the passion of the preceding moments washed away by embarrassment. 'Cy Harding's card,' she said. 'He's promised to make me a model.'

She'd said it cynically, hoping to ease the moment.

'I'll bet he did,' Lee said, a hard expression on his face. 'And, knowing how Cy operates, I guess he put that damned card where I found it?'

'Well. . .yes. . .' Jo felt the accusation of his tone. 'But——'

'But when it's Cy doing the offering it's different,' Lee cut in, his dark brows bristling furiously. 'Because he's going to make you a model—just like your sister. Right?'

Jo shook with temper and with the awful feeling of having lost something which was just within her reach. 'And what's wrong with being a model?' she challenged angrily. 'You fell in love with one. . .'

His hands gripped her arms fiercely, in the now familiar gesture.

'Yeah. That's right—I did. Is that why you want to do it? Are you still bent on offering me what I lost?'

Jo's hand struck out hard and made contact with his cheek.

She flinched, half expecting him to retaliate, but

he gave his head a brief shake, as though dislodging an annoying fly, and she rushed on.

'It seemed to me just now that you were doing the offering,' she cried furiously. 'And as with everything else you've ever offered me, I'm saying no. . .no. . .no!'

Her voice rose almost hysterically and he pulled her into his arms, his mouth silencing her roughly, his kiss no message of love but of aggression and, beneath its power, she felt her strength begin to ebb. Weakly, she clung to him, knowing she would fall if he let go of her now. And subtly his mouth softened on hers, releasing the pent-up tears of frustration. They tasted salt on her lips, and brought a sense of desolation.

At last he lifted his head and put her away from him.

She had hoped to find gentleness in his expression, but, when finally she lifted her eyes to his, she saw only a kind of curiosity.

'To me, that felt more like yes. . .yes. . .yes,' he said sardonically.

She felt like hitting him again, but knew she didn't have the strength to do it.

He took her arm. 'I think it's time we left,' he said.

CHAPTER ELEVEN

Jo did the shopping again with Lee the following morning.

Mo and Stacey had arrived back at the *Ilona* in the early hours of the morning and were still sleeping off the effects of the night before.

Jo, watching Lee's face as he wrote out the list of provisions himself, tried to guess what was going through his mind. His manner with her was quite friendly, but the distance was back between them, as though last night's passion had existed only in a dream. But it hadn't been a dream and the feeling of having been within grasping-point of something wonderful still hung around Jo, making her feel depressed.

Another two days and she would be travelling back home, and in a month's time all this would probably seem as unreal as home did at the moment.

Lee, no doubt, would be glad to see the back of her.

As she wandered around the shopping precinct with him, Jo wondered, for the first time in a long time, where Jocelyn was now. Was she still with Burt Keegan? Or had that romance come to an equally abrupt end? Perhaps her twin had gone home and was, even now, wondering what had become of Jo.

All her thoughts semed to lead to an even deeper sense of depression, and back aboard, engrossed in the routines of getting out of harbour, she decided to enjoy the next two days as they came and put off the thought of leaving until the last possible moment.

Two hours out of harbour the wind had dropped considerably and the sun beat down hot and strong. Jo fetched a blanket to do a little sunbathing. She read for a while and then settled into a comfortable doze.

'Joanne!' Lee called, cutting into her dreamy, sun-induced lethargy. 'Come forward. We're going to hit a rough spot.'

Jo opened her eyes and blinked against the fiercely bright light of a cloudless sky. The sea looked calm and the *Ilona* was steady. No sign anywhere of rough weather.

She shot an indignant glance in Lee's direction, wondering what he was up to now, but he was talking to Mo.

He turned suddenly and caught her glaring at him. 'Come forward quickly and get your jacket.'

His tone was brusquely commanding and Joanne gritted her teeth as she scooped up her blanket and book and made her way towards him. It seemed he was never going to forgive her for just being there.

The deck pitched suddenly. A wave hit starboard, drenching her in spray and sending her sprawling over the edge of the cockpit and into Lee's arms.

For breathless seconds he held her, the wet material of her thin T-shirt clinging to his bare chest, and Jo thought she felt the strong beat of his heart alter pace. Her own heart stopped beating and then began to race.

He put her away impatiently and urged her towards the cabin. 'Go below quickly and change. Put your waterproofs on and bring up the harnesses. I think we'll need them shortly.'

Stumbling below, Jo stifled a wave of nausea. Even the mildest movement of the deck was intensified below and now the yacht was heaving consistently beneath her feet. Lee had been right to forecast rough weather. Did sailors develop some psychic sense about such things?

She put on trousers and a warm sweater, feeling more queasy with every moment, and her fingers were clumsy as she struggled to open the safety catch on the cupboard which held the harnesses.

'Hurry up, Jo,' Lee called. 'I want you up here ready to take the wheel.'

Jo clambered awkwardly up on to the deck and dumped the harnesses on the seat behind Lee. 'In a storm?' she queried incredulously.

He'd insisted on everyone taking their turn at the wheel for practice and Jo had quite enjoyed the experience. She'd been surprised at the comparative ease with which she'd learned to maintain the balance of a steady course. But in these conditions!

'Not a storm,' he corrected calmly. 'We're in an acceleration zone. The wind intensifies in the channel between two islands. The band here isn't a broad one, so it shouldn't last long. It'll provide good practice for you.'

Stacey had come into the cockpit and was handing the harnesses around. 'If she's not up to it, I'll do it,' she offered smugly. She still seemed to have trouble remembering Joanne's name.

'I've asked Jo,' Lee said abruptly. 'We all have to do our share.'

Jo burned inwardly. It hadn't been easy mastering the various routines of sailing, nor the different names and knots for the various ropes, but she'd felt a certain satisfaction in the number of things she had managed. So it was galling to have him talking about her to Stacey as though she was trying to shirk her share of the duties.

She moved to take up her position at the wheel, bracing the back of her legs against the seat behind for support.

'Two hundred and forty west,' Lee said and Jo swung the wheel slowly to the correct position, only to have it almost wrenched from her hand by the next swell.

'Try to keep her steady.'

Jo gritted her teeth. That's what I am trying to do, my dear man, if you did but care to notice, but he had his back to her, pulling up the hood, fastening it tight and Stacey was helping him, standing close and trying to catch his eye.

'Go help Mo bring in some sail,' he told her sharply and her smile disappeared.

How could anyone flounce on a heaving deck? Jo asked herself wryly. But Stacey managed it in spectacular style and Jo saw the momentary flicker of interest on Lee's face as his gaze settled on Stacey's undeniably shapely bottom as it clambered indignantly away from him.

He really was a cool customer, Jo thought, seeing how easily he could switch his feelings on and off. For over a week he and Stacey had danced together, and made love together and he had probably been devastated by his discovery of her unfaithfulness with Mo, and yet his face when he looked at her—his voice when he spoke to her—was completely dispassionate.

The boat dipped suddenly into a deep trough and a surge of nausea hit Jo with unexpected force. She swallowed it back determinedly and rotated the wheel back to its original position.

'Having trouble?' Lee's eyes pierced hers as she turned to look up at him.

She turned quickly away and shook her head. 'I'm all right.'

She felt his continued scrutiny of her face, and sensed rather than saw his irritable frown.

'Did you remember to take your pills?'

Jo nodded affirmatively, unable to speak a direct lie. She'd deliberately not taken them. She'd wanted to test herself on what had seemed a calm day, to see just how far her sea-legs had developed. It had been a mistake, as she now realised, but she wasn't going to confess that to Lee.

'You look a little green about the gills.'

'I'm not surprised,' she acknowledged grimly. 'This is rough. But I dare say I'll survive.'

'Oh, sure. You'll survive.'

To her surprise, he came and stood behind her,

pushing her in towards the wheel, taking the weight of her back against his hard chest, his hands coming around her to grip the wheel, only inches from her own.

All kinds of strange sensations were shooting through her as he braced himself against the seat and drew her more closely against him. The whole length of her body was in contact with his and his warmth penetrated even the thick waterproofs that came between them.

Her knees were in danger of buckling and there was no way she could prevent herself from leaning on him.

'Watch out to port,' he cried suddenly and Jo saw the huge wave crashing towards them.

The boat seemed to shudder with shock as the wave struck and the deck rose steeply. If Lee hadn't been there, she would have fallen. As it happened, drenched and half blinded by the stinging salt water, she grabbed wildly at the wheel and all but wrenched it out of his hands.

She felt the almost superhuman effort Lee made to bring the wheel back, and as the yacht steadied her pushed her quickly aside on to the seat and reached for the automatic pilot.

Mo and Stacey tumbled breathlessly into the cockpit.

'What happened?' Mo's face ran with water.

Lee shrugged. 'Nothing much. Jo isn't feeling too good.'

'I told you it would be better to let me have the

wheel.' Stacey's smug face looked even more beautiful drenched with spray and with long tendrils of blonde hair clinging to her neck and cheeks. 'I don't see the point of putting everyone else's life in danger to teach someone who obviously has no idea, and probably never will have.'

'Thanks for the expert opinion, Stacey,' Lee said drily. 'Fortunately, I was standing by, so you were in no real danger. And since you're still in one piece, you can watch over things here in your expert way, while I take our non-sailor below. She's getting greener by the second.'

Jo listened in a detached way, uncaring of what label they pinned on her. All of her concentration was on keeping her stomach from throwing up its contents.

Lee pulled her to her feet, and she lost the battle. As the boat bucked against a wave crashing head on, she vomited.

Momentary embarrassment was swamped by the certain knowledge that her insides were parting from her body and there wasn't a thing she could do about it.

The next few hours were a hazy nightmare. She vaguely remembered being lifted and carried below, and since it was Lee's face she saw intermittently as a clean bucket was substituted for the one she'd been clinging to in nauseous desperation, she assumed he'd carried her and that it was his hands which, on occasion, gently sponged her forehead and face in tepid water. Gratitude for his unflinching care crept into her consciousness, in between the certainty that she would die and the more terrifying prospect that perhaps she wouldn't.

As dishes and loose objects crashed and slithered about on the deck, Jo gave up the will to live and became weakly resigned to let nature take its course.'

A lifetime later, she became aware of a curious calm. The boat rocked gently as a cradle and the roaring sound of wind and waves had vanished. Was she in heaven? she asked herself before tentatively opening her eyes.

The cabin looked like a battlefield, with things strewn and broken about the place. She was held into the bunk by a cotton harness someone, probably Lee, had put up to prevent her falling out to join the debris on the floor.

The place smelled rancid and unpleasant.

Where was Lee? she wondered, with a surge of embarrassment. Now it was all over, was he disgusted by what he'd been forced to do for her?

She hauled herself into a sitting position and listened. There was no sound from the upper deck and for a moment she almost panicked. Had everyone disappeared overboard in the storm?

With clumsy fingers, she untied the knots holding the harness in place. Her legs seemed to weigh a ton as she dragged them over the side of the bunk and pulled herself upright. Everything spun dizzily around and her knees had turned to jelly.

Jo closed her eyes, praying she wouldn't vomit again. Her stomach was raw and empty but mercifully showed no signs of wanting to retch. Gradually her spinning senses steadied and she was able to pull herself weakly up the steps to the upper deck.

Lee was sittng in the cockpit reading a newspaper. He looked up as her head appeared almost at his feet.

'How do you feel?'

The sky behind him glowed red and gold and reflected colourfully on the water of the harbour, as smooth as a mill-pond.

'I'm not sure yet,' Jo groaned and put a shaking hand to her aching head. 'Where are the others?'

Lee grunted and lowered his gaze once more to his newspaper. 'If it's Mo you're looking for,' he said pointedly, 'he went ashore with Stacey for dinner.'

Jo sat down heavily on the seat opposite Lee, too weak to argue with the obvious jibe about Mo. 'Weren't you hungry?'

He gave a short laugh. 'Ravenous. But someone had to stay aboard and look out for you.'

Jo's pale face flamed. 'I would have been all right as long as you'd told me you were going ashore.' She bit her lip. 'You didn't need to go hungry on my account.'

'I didn't go hungry,' he corrected her drily, and she saw the remains of a salad in the bowl on the small table. 'I grilled myself a steak.'

Jo groaned. 'Oh, please don't mention food.' She rubbed weakly at her still painful stomach. 'I don't think I'll ever eat again.'

He gave an amused laugh. 'I know the feeling,' he said, his voice surprisingly comforting, 'but you'll feel better in an hour or two. There's hot water for a shower.' His eyes held a gleam of what seemed suspiciously like teasing, but Jo dismissed the idea. 'When you're ready, I'll give you a hand.'

Jo's eyes flew open. 'To shower? No, thanks. I think I can manage.'

He was waiting for her as she stepped out from the shower, lounging back in the seat, his dark head buried once again in his newspaper. He looked devastating in tan trousers and a crisp white shirt.

'You feeling OK now?'

Jo nodded, clutching the large bath-square more securely around her. As his dark eyes bored enquiringly into hers, she grew so hot it was a wonder steam didn't rise from her still damp body.

'Good. Then get dressed quickly. We're going ashore.'

It wasn't until they were seated together in a long, low silver limousine and cruising noiselessly away from the quayside that Jo found her voice.

'Where are we going?'

He gave her a brief, amused glance. 'Don't worry. You're not being kidnapped.'

Jo flushed. 'I didn't think I was. But I would still like to know where you're taking me.'

'I've got a place west of here. I thought a spell of landlubber comfort might do you good after your shake-up.'

'Oh! I see,' she answered doubtfully.

'No, you don't.' He surprised her with a dry laugh. 'But you will.'

His 'place' was a house right on the beach, with a

long, low veranda facing the sea. A Spanish-type
paved garden, shaded by broad-leaf trees and hung
with flowers, led around to the rear.

Jo was awestruck. 'It's wonderful.'

'Glad you like it.' Lee guided her towards the
front entrance. 'It was always my favourite place.'

And Jo wasn't surprised, except by how easily he
took beautiful things for granted.

Once inside, he ushered her into a large living-
room, with a huge window taking up the whole of
one wall and giving a panoramic view of the sea.

'I wired ahead to have some food brought in. Are
you hungry?'

Jo shook her head. 'No. But I'd love a cup of tea.'

Lee nodded. 'OK, I'll see if we can oblige.'

A shadow flitted across the room and, looking out
of the window, Jo saw a great bank of grey clouds
gathering around the lowering sun. She shivered in
the sudden chill.

Lee shrugged out of his jacket. 'I'll be a few
minutes in the kitchen,' he said. 'And when I come
back I'll light the fire, since you're obviously cold.'

'Oh, no! Please! I'm not really cold. It was only a
momentary shiver when the sun went in.'

He laughed shortly. 'It'll be going in for good
soon, so we'll need the fire.'

'We won't be stopping that long,' Jo argued. 'So
it won't be worth the bother.'

With a start, she realised he was watching her, his
dark eyes quizzical. 'It's no bother,' he said drily.
'And how long we stay depends on the storm that's
brewing. The way the wind's rising. . .' He shook

his head. 'It could last for a couple of hours, or a couple of days.'

Jo's mouth dropped open. 'A couple of days? But that means we'll be. . .' She broke off, a dull flush beginning in her throat.

'Marooned alone together in the house?' he finished for her and then laughed. 'Don't worry. Mo and Stacey will be along some time later. Meanwhile, I'll try not to compromise you.'

Jo sighed inwardly, grateful for his assurance, laconically given, but none the less dependable. . . she hoped. Because if he were to try to make love to her here in this beautiful house, away from everyone, she couldn't guarantee she wouldn't succumb.

Then she groaned as she remembered something else. . .something she'd been forcing out of her mind for some time. 'I have to be at the airport the day after next for my return flight. Do you think I'll make it?'

He shrugged. 'Just keep your fingers crossed this storm blows over,' he said. 'But for now there's nothing we can do about anything, so we'll cross that bridge when we come to it.' He set light to the log fire in the wide stone grate and brought a low table to the settee. 'I'll go and get the tea. Be back soon. Make yourself at home.'

Jo prowled about the beautiful room, her hands trailing over the lovely fabrics, the sturdy polished wood, thinking it would be wonderful to spend some time here.

But the realisation that she would be leaving soon

dampened her spirits. In the circumstances, she thought ironically, she might almost be glad to see Cy Harding walking in through the door with the offer of a job in modelling. If he was genuine, at least it would mean she could stay in the area and perhaps see Lee from time to time. But that would be torture, after all. No. It would be better for her to go home, far away from the reminders of the man who had stolen her heart and peace of mind— perhaps forever.

She groaned, seeing clearly what lay ahead. The mundane occupation of secretary had lost its appeal and the thought of having to search for a new job as soon as she arrived home just added to her depression.

She was still moving restlessly about the room when Lee came back with a tray.

He kicked the low table nearer to the deeply cushioned settee. 'Sit down,' he ordered. 'Now your stomach's settled, you'll be able to eat. I hope you like scrambled egg.'

As soon as she saw the dainty triangles of thin toast and fluffy yellow eggs she was suddenly ravenous. Her stomach seemed cavernously empty and she ate every scrap from the plate with real enjoyment.

He was looking at her with wry amusement as she finished the last mouthful. She'd been so engrossed in the food she had almost forgotten his existence.

'I didn't realise I was so hungry,' she said with a slight flush staining her cheeks. 'Was I making a pig of myself?'

He shook his head. 'It's a relief to know I can give you something without having it flung straight back at me. I'd hate to have egg on my face.'

Jo laughed at the small pun and her flush deepened. 'I suppose I must have seemed very ungrateful at times?'

He nodded. 'Uh-huh.'

She smiled at him, loving the crinkling of the skin around his eyes as he answered her with a grin. Now that she was leaving, it seemed possible for them to lower the barriers between them.

'I didn't mean to be, you know,' she said apologetically. 'It was self-defence. You were equally pig-headed in believing I was out to get everything I could from you.'

He shrugged. 'I guess it's what I'm used to.'

'No,' she argued gently. 'It's what you expect. . .and perhaps sometimes you force people to live up to your expectations.'

'Maybe.' He shook his head musingly. 'Never thought of it in quite that light before.'

He was sitting in the corner angle of the settee, his long legs stretched out before him, his arm slung comfortably along the back, more relaxed than she had ever seen him.

She found herself wishing, achingly, that she was nestled in the crook of his arm instead of a mile away at the opposite end of the large settee. Careful, she chided herself. Don't be fooled into thinking this cosy camaraderie will last—it never has. But it was lovely while it lasted.

'By the way, thanks for looking after me when I

was seasick.' It was even possible to mention that without embarrassment and she'd been wanting him to know she was grateful.

'Don't mention it. I won't say it was a pleasure—tending the seasick is never that—but it was a necessity. Somebody had to take care of you.'

The gentle, teasing voice, the words themselves, brought a lump to Jo's throat.

'It meant a lot to me,' she admitted softly. 'Nobody's taken care of me in a long, long time.' As soon as she said it, she wished she hadn't. 'I didn't mean to sound sorry for myself,' she rushed in defensively. 'It's just that being a child, and all that means, seems such a long time ago. My father died when I was ten and for the last two years of my mother's life she was practically bed-ridden and it was I who had to care for her.'

'Just you?' Lee queried. 'No help from Jocelyn?'

She was surprised at how easily he said her sister's name, but there was censure in his tone.

'She was in London making a career for herself,' she said, sounding a little defensive. 'She was too busy to keep running back and forth, whereas I was on the spot.'

Lee's mouth curved cynically. 'Yeah! Literally!'

Jo shrugged. She wished now that she hadn't started this conversation, but she had to go on because he seemed to think she was blaming her sister for the way things were, and it simply wasn't the case.

'When Mother died, I got the house. Jocelyn relinquished her half to me.' Jo felt some satisfaction in telling him that. 'Jocelyn's always been self-centred and wayward, but never grasping.'

Surely he would concede that when he thought of all the clothes he'd bought for her, but which she'd willingly left behind.

'Her career as a model was going well,' Jo continued. 'She had her own flat in London and saw no point in taking half the house from me.'

Lee snorted. 'You see that as something in her favour?' he demanded. 'She gets to go off without any responsibility—leaving you behind to carry the can—and you feel lucky she let you have the house?'

'No—no,' Jo cried defensively but with spirit. 'It wasn't like that. My mother was a wonderful woman. She bore everything with courage. She was never the complaining invalid.' Jo felt the lump in her throat grow bigger, almost to the point of choking her. 'And besides,' she whispered raggedly around the constriction, 'I wanted to care for her. I loved her. . .'

She stopped, because, for the moment, it was impossible to go on.

The sky had grown very dark, casting deep shadows into the room, relieved only by the flicker of dancing flames from the log fire. Jo stared into them, waiting for the pain of remembering to subside.

Lee leaned forward unexpectedly to brush her hair back from her face. 'Baby,' he said tenderly, 'don't get sad. It's all in the past and you know you did your best.'

Jo swallowed the lump and fought back the tears.

Yes. She'd done her best and her mother had died peacefully, knowing Jo loved her. Jocelyn had been the unlucky one—she hadn't been there at the end to hold her mother's hand. . .

'Could I borrow your hanky?' she asked huskily.

He took the immaculate square from his shirt pocket and handed it to her. 'Have a good blow.'

His down-to-earth command brought a smile to her lips. 'Yes, sir,' she said and blew hard.

He took it from her and turned a clean corner to wipe her eyes, tossing it into the flames when he'd finished.

Jo's frugal upbringing rebelled against such waste until she remembered he could afford the gesture.

'That's better,' he said. 'Gee! You look beautiful when you cry and I don't know many women who can say that.'

Jo bit her lip, fighting a sudden stab of jealousy. 'And I expect you know a lot of women,' she said, in an attempt at teasing, hoping he wouldn't notice the pain of her expression.

'No maybe about that,' he admitted. 'Too many of the wrong kind.' His voice softened. 'But I've got a feeling right now that my luck's about to change at last.'

He turned her face up to his and held her gaze openly. Jo's eyes widened. There was no help for it now because her heart was in them, telling him everything he wanted to know.

He put his lips on hers, softly, sensuously, drawing the very heart out of her body, and her hands went out to hold him.

With a rough little cry, he drew her into his arms. She lifted her face to him, but he didn't kiss her, simply tucking her head into the hollow of his shoulder as he cradled her.

'Hell, Jo! You feel so good, woman,' he said. 'Soft. . .yelding. . .the way a woman ought to be.'

'But not submissive,' she lifted her head to argue.

He laughed. 'Don't I know it.'

He pushed her head back and his arms tightened about her as though he would never let her go, thrilling her in a way no other embrace ever had.

With her head against him like this, she could hear the strong rhythmic beat of his heart and was close to a kind of ecstasy. A strange pain was tearing through her. She was here in his arms where she had wanted to be for so long and it hurt not to know whether she really belonged there. Was this sympathy? Or love?

With a little sob, she turned her head to kiss the strong column of his throat, pressing her mouth hungrily against the firm, smooth skin, and his hold tightened convulsively, almost breaking her bones.

Then he was shaking her away from him, staring intently down into her misty eyes. 'Jo. I've been trying for a long time to be good with you,' he said raggedly. 'This time I want to make sure you're ready. But I can't hold out forever.'

He took her hand and held it against him, the way he had that first night in the study, making her know the power of his feelings.

'I want you, Jo. . .and. . .lord. . .how I need

you,' he said, low and husky. 'But only when you're ready.'

With a feeling that she was jumping off a precipice, Jo reached up and drew his lips down to hers. Whatever this passion was that burned within him, her searing, melting body matched it. . .and she could no longer turn away.

'I love you, Lee,' she said.

A loud crack of thunder rent the air as though confirming her simple statement for all eternity.

The rain came down and the wind blew a gale outside, but Jo was transported in Lee's arms to another world—a world of ecstasy and consummation, of peace and comfort, and of coming home. . .

Nobody came through the storm to disturb them and later Lee carried her up to bed and made love to her all over again.

The rain had stopped when Jo woke.

It took a moment or two for her to remember where she was, her body seeming to feel the sway of the yacht beneath her, even through her memory told her she was on dry land. When the other memories came flooding back, a mixture of emotions took over.

Gingerly, she reached out a hand to explore the other side of the bed, but it was empty and she sighed with relief. She wasn't sure yet that she could cope with seeing Lee, and her stomach churned as she wondered what his attitude would be to what had happened between them the night before.

Would he imagine that she'd planned it. . .led him on?

Would he regret it?

Worse! Had he been thinking of Jocelyn when he was loving her?

Oh, lord, no! That would be too much to bear.

She had woken some time during the night and reached for him and he had gathered her against him, nestling her head in the hollow of his shoulder, cradling her as he had earlier, and she had slept again with a contentment she had never before known.

She threw back the bedclothes and rose, shocked to discover that she was stark naked. They had undressed each other last night in the living-room and her clothes must be strewn about there as evidence of an abandon, the memory of which now took her breath away.

She got up quickly and found a bathrobe in the wardrobe. Obviously Lee's, it buried her from head to toe, but would afford her some decency until she could bath and recover her clothes.

A thin, watery sun was up, trying to dry out the sodden earth. The wind hadn't dropped altogether. It capped the huge waves with brilliant white as they came crashing on to the rain-hardened beach and Jo gasped as she saw Lee swimming in on the crest of one of the monsters.

She was dressed and cooking breakfast when he came into the kitchen, wrapped in a towelling robe, his thick hair dripping salt water everywhere. She kept her face averted, pretending to be engrossed in the business of frying bacon and eggs.

She couldn't bear to look at him. . .afraid she might see the regret—or, perhaps worse, the disgust—he might be feeling about the way she had abandoned all modesty and made love with him last night—and not just once. . .

He dropped a cold, wet kiss on the back of her neck and she felt her spirits rise. He hadn't rejected her.

'Beast. I've just had a shower,' she joked to cover the loud hammering of her heartbeat.

'Spoilsport,' he said teasingly. 'I was hoping we'd have one together.'

He stood behind her, his hands leaning on the stove, one each side of her, and she could smell the tangy salt spray, feel the damp heat of him, and her insides began the familiar churning.

'Go away,' she said firmly as she turned the bacon with a spatula. 'I'm too busy to be bothered by you.'

He dropped another kiss on her neck and stood back. 'That's not what you said last night,' he quipped.

Jo put down the spatula and turned within the circle of his arms, unable any longer to keep from reading his eyes.

They were smiling at her, dark and inviting, reviving memories of the ecstasy they had held out to her the night before.

'Good morning, my wild English rose,' he said, suddenly intense. 'No regrets?'

Jo started at his words, an echo of her own

thoughts of only moments ago. She shook her head and lowered her eyes. 'None.'

'That's good.' He lifted her chin. 'You should have told me it was the first time, Jo.'

Her startled eyes flew up and hot colour mounted her cheeks. The truth was, their coming together had been so natural, so wonderful, that there had been nothing in her mind but the ecstasy of the moment.

'I didn't think. . .' she muttered, biting her soft lower lip. 'What difference would it have made?'

He cupped her face. 'All the difference in the world. I could have made it easier for you. . .better. . .'

She shook her head, wanting to tell him nothing could ever be easier or better than the loving he had given her, but it went too deep, too intimate for her to share. . .even with him.

'Your bacon's burning,' she said, deliberately tearing her eyes away and turning back to the stove.

'I take the hint,' he said, dropping a kiss on her head. 'But only for now. And the next time won't be. . .the first—nor the last.'

Mercifully, he'd turned away before the tremor inside her grew to a quake.

'I'll go shower,' he said. 'Don't go away. I'll be right back.'

Her heart was singing. She had more than half anticipated things would have changed. That he would be back to the cool, critical Lee she'd come to know so well these past days and she didn't know how she would have coped with that. To have him teasing and affectionate and obviously regretting nothing made her feel so good it hurt.

He wasn't gone long and came back showered and dressed and looking more handsome than ever. 'Mmm. That smells delicious.'

She laid a place for him at the table and put food on a plate for him. 'A good old-fashioned English breakfast.'

'Followed by a good old-fashioned English girl.' He kissed her briefly on the lips before seating himself and picking up his knife and fork. 'But first things first.'

'You look a little tired. Why don't you just relax there while I take a look at the mail?'

Lee had cooked lunch and they'd eaten it in front of the fire. It had begun to rain shortly afterwards and the wind was rising again in force.

Mo and Stacey still hadn't arrived and nothing had been said about Jo's return flight the following day. She'd been deliberately trying to keep the thought from her mind, but it was something she would have to face shortly because her clothes were still on the yacht and would need to be collected before she went home.

The fact that Lee hadn't mentioned it either seemed to her to mean he had no alternative in mind. But then, why should he have? It was she who had spoken to him of love. No such word had passed his lips in the loving moments of last night or this morning after breakfast.'

Jo sighed. 'I think I will.'

Lee turned on a small lamp and sat in its light quietly opening the envelopes he'd picked up from the small harbour post office the evening before on the way out, his face alert and absorbed as he scanned the contents of one letter after another.

Jo, lying back with her eyes half closed, took the opportunity of observing him unnoticed as his attention remained wholly on what he was reading.

He had a lean, forceful face, his skin smooth and firm, but there were lines etched deeply each side of his mouth as he pulled his lips into a straight thin line. One letter was definitely disturbing him and Jo wondered what it could be to bring such a deep frown to his dark brow.

He looked up suddenly and saw her looking at him. 'If you'll excuse me, I have a few phone calls to make before this storm takes hold and maybe cuts out the line.' He put the letters from him and stood up abruptly. 'I'll be back in a little while.'

He left the room and Jo wondered if he had a study here too. He'd obviously arranged for his mail to be forwarded on to him even when he was on holiday.

Without him, the room seemed suddenly empty. She was wide awake now and moved forward to pour herself a cup of tea from the tall pot keeping warm on a hotplate. The movement displaced some of the papers Lee had left lying on the cushioned seat and they went fluttering to the ground.

With a little cry of exasperation, she bent down to pick them up and was surprised to find that one of the letters was written in familiar handwriting.

Her pulse quickened and her mouth went suddenly very dry.

The letter belonged to Lee. . .a private message to him from the person who had written it. She had no right to read it, no matter how much she might long to know what Jocelyn had to say to her fiancé, and firmly she put it among the other letters on the settee without looking at it further.

But it was impossible for her to sit quietly now. Lee had gone off to telephone and no doubt Jocelyn would turn up here sooner or later to make her own peace with him. Hopefully, it wouldn't be until after she had gone home. As much as she had wanted to help Jocelyn and Lee get back together again, if that was what they both wanted, things had changed drastically now, and she couldn't bear the thought of being around when the reconciliation took place.

She couldn't even bear to be in the house now. The peacefulness of this room was shattered by her own tumultuous thoughts, its warmth, its memories tarnished by the realisation that she had made love not to a free man, but to her sister's fiancé.

The heat from the fire was suddenly overwhelming.

Out of doors, with the wind tearing through her hair and tugging at her clothes, she knew a sense of panic. She would have to leave quickly. There was no way she could spend another night with Lee, having to keep herself at arm's length from him, remembering every wonderful touch of his body, his hands against her, and knowing he was forever outside of her reach.

The rain which had been thin and gusting turned torrential, drenching her through in a matter of seconds. The wet sand oozed puddles which filled her shoes and made it difficult for her to walk, but she was only dimly aware of her discomfort. There was far more than discomfort in her heart. It felt as though it were being wrenched in two. Her love for Lee told her she must stay and fight, however small the chance of winning, but loyalty, bred in her shared genes, forbade her to take what might still belong to her twin.

She began to run, with no sense of direction, and no destination. And she didn't stop when she found herself running towards the crashing surf.

'Joanne!' She heard Lee's call behind her and turned to see him, running to catch up with her.

Doggedly, she increased her speed, stopping momentarily to tear the waterlogged shoes from her feet, fearful that if he caught up with her—held her—she might break down and beg him. . .

She was at the water's edge now and the only way forward was across the jutting rocks. Stopping only to tie her skirt about her thighs, she went on, slipping and slithering across the seemingly endless expanse of gleaming wet stone.

Lee's arms came about her as she teetered on the edge of an abyss she didn't have the strength to jump. He was panting almost as heavily as she, and she could feel the pounding beat of his heart as he pulled her against him.

'You idiot!' he shouted above the roar of the water. 'What do you think you're doing?'

'Let me go!' she yelled back, beginning to struggle in his grasp. 'Go. . .back to. . . Jocelyn. . .'

But he held on to her grimly, his face pale and running with water, which dashed with ominous force against the rocks.

Her breathing was short and laboured and she summoned the last of her failing strength to push at him. 'Go back to her. . .where you belong.'

The final push dislodged his hold and he staggered back, slithering about on the treacherous stones, his hands waving like windmills as he tried to regain his balance.

Before Jo's horrified gaze, he went down, and above the crashing roar of the waves she heard the sound his head made when it came into contact with the rocks.

For long seconds she stood frozen, petrified by horror and a terrible fear. He lay unmoving as torrents of water splashed and ebbed around him. The only movement was his clothes as the water began to lift and drag him towards the edge of the rocks.

Suddenly, she sprang into life.

'Lee!' she screamed. 'Oh, no! Lee! I've killed you!'

With desperate hands, she clutched at his clothing, pulling with all her new-found strength to bring him away from the danger. Perhaps he wasn't dead. . . only stunned.

'God!' she prayed aloud. 'Please don't let him be dead. Please! Please! Don't punish me this way.'

Slowly, painfully, she brought him towards her,

his body, limp and lifeless, weighing even more heavily because of his water-sodden clothes. Pain tore at her arms and hands as she strained and she could feel herself weakening. She relinquished her hold for seconds while she stood up and stretched her pain-racked body and the water rushed in, reclaiming the ground she had so painfully won.

Her scream rang out, echoing in her head louder than the elements, and a terrible blackness seemed about to engulf her.

'Don't let me faint!' she screamed. 'Oh, God! I mustn't faint.'

She bent again to clutch Lee's clothes, but strong arms were pulling her back, lifting her away. She struggled like a woman demented until she saw Mo's face close to her own.

'It's all right, Jo. I'll get him.'

He relinquished her sagging body into other arms and Jo hazily recognised Stacey's rain-soaked and beautiful face before the world slipped away.

CHAPTER TWELVE

It was Mo who was bending over Jo when she came round.

A grin of relief split his broad face as her eyes opened. 'Just lie still awhile. You'll be all right.'

Memory came rushing back. 'Lee!' she cried, struggling to sit up in the bed. 'Is he dead?'

Mo pushed her gently but firmly back. 'Hell, no! It will take more than a little knock on the head to kill Lee. But he's still groggy. The doctor's on his way.'

'If he dies. . . I'll never forgive myself,' she said shakily. She buried her face in the pillow and began to sob.

'He's not going to die,' Mo said, suddenly impatient. 'Pull yourself together, Jo. This doesn't help anyone.' But his hand was gentle as he stroked her head. 'Come on, now. This isn't like you.'

Jo sniffed back her tears and sat up slowly. 'But you don't understand, Mo. It was all my fault. I pushed him.'

'Then you probably had good reason,' he said philosophically. 'But you can straighten all that out when you see him later.'

Jo's insides clenched sickeningly and she knew she couldn't face seeing Lee now. If she once saw what she'd done to him she would never be able to leave,

164

and that was something she just had to do. . .for both their sakes.

'Mo,' she said urgently, 'I've got to get back to the yacht to pick up my clothes. I'm leaving for home tomorrow.'

Mo's fair brows rose. 'Home! Surely you can't be thinking of that now? Wait and see what Lee has to say once the doctor's been.'

Jo recoiled. To wait and see what Lee had to say was the last thing in the world she wanted to do. What could he say? Sorry! It was all a mistake! I didn't know Jocelyn was coming back!

She knew him well enough now to know he would feel responsible for her. He might even offer her money as a consolation and that would be unbearable.

'No. I can't wait.' Jo shook her head vigorously. 'If I miss my flight tomorrow, I may not be able to get another one for days, perhaps weeks, and I've got to get home.'

She pushed back the covers and was surprised to find she was wearing a man's pyjamas, several sizes too large. Someone had taken her wet clothes from her body. Her eyes flew questioningly to Mo's.

'Stacey,' he supplied in answer to her unspoken query. 'I swear!' He lifted his hand. 'She wouldn't let me touch you.' He gave her a wry grin.

'Oh, Mo!' she wailed. 'I'm in no mood for humour.'

Jocelyn might be on her way here right now and Jo was in no state of mind to meet up with her twin.

It would be better all round if she simply disappeared out of sight, out of mind and left the way clear for them to reconcile their differences.

She tried to feel happy for them both, but felt only bitter desolation.

If only she hadn't come here. If only he hadn't made love to her, she might have been able to bear the thought of them back together again. At the moment, it seemed impossible. But perhaps—back home—with the past weeks behind her and the memories beginning to fade, she might gradually come to terms with her loss.

'I need my clothes,' she said, her voice sounding a little desperate. 'I want to leave as quickly as possible.'

'OK, OK,' Mo soothed her. 'They're in the machine. I don't suppose they'll take long.' He frowned hard at her. 'But Lee isn't going to like this.'

He left and Jo went into the bathroom. There was no time for a shower—a wash would have to do.

She washed her face and ran a comb through her hair. Her handbag was still in the living-room so she would have to forgo her make-up. She looked pale, despite her tan, and her eyes were huge and glassy, but what did it matter?

Mo came back with a petulant Stacey carrying Jo's clothes.

'What am I supposed to be? Some kind of lady's maid or something?' she grumbled.

To Jo's surprise, Mo just grinned and hugged her. 'I'll make it up to you later, honey. I promise.'

Stacey tossed her head at him. 'Big deal.'

She ignored Jo completely, simply turning her back to leave the room. Mo tapped her shapely bottom as she stalked away.

Jo had no time to wonder about his apparent light-heartedness. Her mind was full of only one idea: to get away as quickly as possible—without Lee knowing. . .

Mo grumbled as he turned his car in the drive, and Stacey's face was furious as they drove away from the house. She'd been instructed by Mo to stay with Lee and to take careful note of what the doctor said about his condition.

At the last moment, Jo had almost been unable to leave for worry about him. 'Are you sure he'll be all right?' she enquired anxiously.

'I'm sure. He'll have a sore head for a while, I guess, but he's had more than one of those before.'

Perhaps she should have seen him for herself. It might have put her mind at rest, but it would have broken her heart.

She settled back into the seat and tried to calm her frayed nerves, but the picture of Lee's body slipping slowly into the sea kept rising to haunt her.

'Thank goodness you came in time, Mo,' she said, as he turned the car out of the track and on to the coast road. 'Any later and we might both have gone into the sea.'

'Yeah. We saw you come out of the house just as we were coming up the track. And then a little later Lee came out and you started to run. We thought it was some kind of private fight so we kept out of it until we saw you running towards the sea.' He shot her a quick glance. 'What were you trying to do, Jo? Were things that bad?'

Jo stared at him, puzzled, and then realisation dawned. 'Did you think. . .?' She shook her head. 'Oh, no! I was just running. . . I didn't even notice. . .' Her voice had begun to rise.

'OK, OK. Forget it,' Mo said.

Had Lee thought she'd been trying. . .? Oh, lord! What a mess. If only. . .

'Where were you yesterday, Mo?' she asked. 'If only you'd come yesterday. . .'

If he'd come yesterday, Lee wouldn't have made love to her. . .she would never have dared hope. . .and Jocelyn's return would have been a little easier to bear. . .

'I was busy.' He flashed her a quick grin. 'Getting married.'

'Married?' Jo echoed in amazement. 'To whom?'

He laughed. 'To Stacey, that's whom.'

'Stacey!'

'Yeah! She decided to cut her losses and say yes.'

Jo was speechless with surprise. So Lee had lost another of his women. Not that it would be important now. The only woman who mattered to him was coming back.

'Well,' Mo prompted, 'aren't you going to congratulate me? It is customary.'

'Oh, Mo! I do congratulate you. But. . .are you sure?'

He gave a cheerful snort. 'Too late now if I'm not.'

'I'm sorry,' Jo said contritely. 'I meant. . .'

'I know exactly what you meant.' He smiled. 'Don't worry. Stacey and I are two of a kind. When I've broken her to the rope, we'll get along fine.'

I hope so, Jo muttered silently. The news was startling—confusing—but she had no time to think about it now. They'd arrived at the harbour. . .and the yacht.

'Are you sure you don't want me to wait and take you to the airport?' Mo asked.

'And have Stacey hopping mad about being left alone on her honeymoon, while you spend the night with me?'

Mo grinned. 'Perhaps you're right. But I could come back tomorrow.'

'No. Please. I'll spend the night aboard and go straight to the airport in the morning. It will be easier for everyone that way. Don't worry.'

He thought about it for a while and then shrugged. 'If that's the way you want it.'

'Thanks, Mo.' Jo sighed with relief. 'And thank you for everything else too.'

He shrugged, lifting his broad shoulders. 'What can I say?' He enveloped her in a warm hug. 'Except that I'll miss you.'

Jo felt the tears springing to her eyes. Hearing him say that really brought it home. She was leaving. . .and she would never see him or Lee again. . .

'You'd better go—before I start to cry,' she said, pushing him away. 'Take care of Lee for me.'

'Sure,' he said. 'What shall I tell him?'

She bit her lip. 'Tell him. . .'

She paused. There were so many things she

wished she could say to Lee, only now he wouldn't want to hear them. She felt suddenly glad that she had told him she loved him. At least that was something she wouldn't have to keep secret in her heart.

'Just tell him I said goodbye.'

The yacht was depressingly empty.

Jo put her few things into the holdall Lee had given her and made herself a cup of coffee in the galley, taking it up on deck.

The storm had blown itself out and the sky was a pale watery blue, with thin wispy clouds obscuring the sun. The horizon was yellow and dusky pink and Jo thought it would be a beautiful day tomorrow.

But she wouldn't be here to see it and, back home, she wouldn't care if the skies stayed grey forever. They would match the greyness in her heart.

She wondered how Lee was, and prayed that Mo was right in his assessment of the likely damage from his fall.

'Hi, there. How're you doing, sweetie?'

Jo came out of her reverie with a start, to see Cy Harding waving at her from the quayside.

She sighed. He was the last person in the world she wanted to see right now.

'Permission to come aboard?' he called. 'I really would like to speak with you.' He was tugging the small dinghy ashore.

'No!' Jo called in alarm. 'Please leave that. I'm coming ashore. I have to get to the airport tonight.'

The lie meant she would have to come off the

yacht, but that was better than having to cope here alone with Cy Harding in a pushy mood.

She tossed her cup overboard and rushed to the rope to pull the dinghy back. She tied it firmly to the rail.

'I just have to get my baggage.'

She went below, gathering up her things as quickly as she could, desperate to get ashore in case he found a way of getting out to the yacht.

She had hoped that when she came back up on deck he might have gone, but knew it was a forlorn hope. Resignedly, she tossed her things into the dinghy and climbed in after them.

'Just sit tight and I'll haul you across,' Cy shouted as she released the rope from the rail.

With a sigh, she did just that.

Now the decision to leave was made, she felt a little better. Her stomach felt hollow and she realised that it was hours since she'd last eaten. She would find somewhere to eat and then take a taxi to the airport. She'd spent little of her money and what was left after she'd paid for a meal would more than cover the fare.

'Thank you,' she said, as Cy handed her ashore. 'But really, Mr Harding, there's not much point in talking about anything—I'm going back home.'

'Fine, fine,' he said, picking up her bag and taking her arm. 'But let's just talk about it, shall we? Just talk about it.'

Jo wondered if he ever listened to a word anyone said. 'There's no point,' she said, as he led her along the harbour. 'And where are you taking me?' She stopped and tried to pull her arm free.

'Anywhere you want to go, sweetie.'

Jo wished he'd stop calling her that, but what was the point of arguing the issue now?

His grip tightened on her arm. 'Where would you like to go?'

Looking into his sly, handsome face, Jo knew there was absolutely nowhere she wanted to go with Cy Harding.

'I've already told you—I'm going to the airport.'

She would forgo a meal for now, find a taxi as quickly as possible, and eat when she got there. The sooner she got rid of this annoying little man, the better.

'That's fine,' he said. 'We can talk on the way.'

He was steering her along the harbour again and Jo found herself wondering how on earth she had got herself into this predicament. It might have been better to have stayed on board, out of his reach; cut the dinghy rope if necessary. But then, he wasn't the type to be deterred. Even if it meant he had to swim, she felt certain he would have got to her somehow.

The harbour master passed, tipping his cap to Jo, and she fought down an urge to call out to him. What could she tell him—that Cy Harding was insisting on escorting her to the airport?

Calm down, my girl, she told herself. Your nerves are beginning to get the better of you.

'If you'd just call me a taxi, I'd be very grateful,' she said wearily.

'A taxi,' he laughed. 'Do you have any idea how

far away the airport is? You'd do better to buy the taxi than pay for one.' He was leading her through the car park to a long black limousine. 'Relax. I've got the car right here, so why don't we just travel in comfort?'

'Perhaps I could get a bus,' Jo said a trifle desperately. He had the door open and she had an awful feeling he would win in the end.

'You would need several buses, and at this time of the evening there are just none around,' he said, with an edge of exasperation. He indicated the car. 'If you don't want to get in that's fine, but I'm just trying to help you, sweetie. Is there anything wrong with that?'

He sounded hurt and Jo felt momentarily sorry. 'No. Of course not. It's really kind of you, but——'

'Well, that's fine. Fine. So why not get in and quit fighting me? I'll take you to the airport.' He gestured towards the back seat. 'Get in the back if it will make you feel any better and I promise I won't say a word until we get there. Not a word.'

Jo suddenly felt bone-weary. Tired. . .hungry. . . and defeated. She needed to get to the airport, and the sooner she arrived the better it would be. And, since he'd offered her the back seat, she would take it.

'OK,' she said at last. 'And thank you very much.'

Jo hadn't thought she'd sleep. With all the happenings of the day and her anxieties about Lee, she hadn't expected to be able to even close her eyes. But she had.

The big car was comfortable and warm and she'd been worn out and she'd obviously been dozing for some time. It was dark now and, apart from the lighted roadway ahead, there was nothing to be seen through the car windows.

'Are we nearly there?' Jo asked drowsily.

Cy's eyes met hers in the driving-mirror. 'Not yet. There's a little while to go yet. What time's your flight?'

'Twelve noon tomorrow,' Jo said and she saw his brows rise.

'Tomorrow—then what the hell's the hurry?'

Jo bit her lip, wishing now that she'd told him a lie and said midnight—or two in the morning—but she didn't know the time and he might very well have told her she'd already missed her flight and insisted on taking her back.

'I just want to get to the airport,' she said, on a note of panic.

'Relax. Relax,' he said calmly. 'We'll get there. Just go back to sleep and I'll call you.'

The next time she woke, the car was stopped and she heaved a deep sigh of relief. They'd arrived at last. She sat up, surprised to find the car was empty. Where was Cy? The question was answered a moment later as the door opened and he was beckoning her out.

'Let's go get ourselves something to eat,' he said.

Jo looked at him warily. 'Where are we?'

'Come out and take a look. Come on out, sweetie. I'm starving.'

Jo's stomach was empty too. Just the mention of

food had it rumbling. But she was reluctant to get out of the car.

It was dark all around, as though they were in the heart of the country, and the building in front of them was unlighted, except for one room just ahead.

A man stepped out of the door, dangling a key in his bony hand. His face, peering in at her, looked grubby and disgruntled, and his hair stood on end, as though he'd been woken from his sleep.

'Take number fourteen,' the man said. 'And I'll bring you over a sandwich and some coffee.'

'Come on, now.' Cy reached into the car and grabbed her arm.

She clambered out, stiff from sleeping, and looked about her. 'What is this place?'

'A motel, lady,' the man said. 'You drunk or somethin'?'

'Come on,' Cy said again, and this time his voice had a hard edge. 'Driving all this way. . . I've just got to have a rest and something to eat.'

It sounded reasonable enough, and Jo went, still reluctant but admitting he was entitled to rest and eat.

He relinquished his hold on her at the door of a chalet-like building, snapped on a light and shoved her in before him. The room held two armchairs, a bed and a rickety table.

'Not exactly the Ritz,' Cy said. 'But it'll do. It'll do.'

Jo, feeling more anxious by the minute, wondered what it would do for. 'I don't think I want to stay here,' she said. 'Couldn't we find a restaurant or something?'

He laughed. 'Out here? At three in the morning? You're kidding.'

'No, I'm not kidding.' She was starting to get angry. 'I'd prefer to wait until we reach the airport. There's bound to be a place to eat there.'

Cy was taking off his jacket. 'Right now, sweetie, I don't really care what you'd prefer.' He threw his jacket on to the bed. 'Why don't you just sit down and make yourself comfortable?'

Jo sat gingerly on the edge of one dusty chair, while he went to answer a knock on the door. It was the man with the sandwiches and, as he peered curiously past Cy to Jo, she had a strong urge to rush over and ask him to call her a taxi, but it seemed foolish. Cy had done nothing but remove his jacket and ask her to sit down. The food he had told her he'd stopped to obtain was there on a tray. She was simply being hysterical.

The door closed and her chance was gone.

Cy handed her a plate of sandwiches. 'Eat!' he commanded. 'You'll feel better.'

He sat down in the other chair and wolfed down his share of the food. He really had been hungry after all. Jo began to relax a little.

'How far are we from the airport?'

Cy shrugged. 'An hour or so.'

She stared at him. 'That long?'

The journey was much longer than she had thought. The trip down from Lee's house hadn't seemed that long, but, added to the trip to the airport, she supposed it was about right. She laughed wryly to herself to think she'd been going to hire a taxi. It would have cost the earth. Just as well Cy had come along and offered a lift, or she might have found herself in a very embarrassing situation.

Not that her present situation wasn't embarrassing enough.

Cy was pouring himself another cup of coffee and she wished there was some way she could hurry him up.

But he was taking off his shoes and socks and looked ready to make himself comfortable for some time.

'Cy, please. Couldn't we go now? I'm sorry to rush you, but I'd feel better if we just went.'

'Oh, sure,' he said. 'And what about me? You've had a nice comfortable ride in my nice comfortable car, and all I've had from you is gripe, gripe, gripe.' He reached down and gripped her arms, drawing her to her feet. 'Isn't it about time you started showing me some of that gratitude you were telling me about?'

Jo's heart began to thump. This close, with his eyes narrowed and his lips drawn into a thin line, he looked a cold and dangerous man.

CHAPTER THIRTEEN

'I MEANT what I said, sweetie. I really can get you into modelling.'

Cy Harding was looking at Jo with that awful assessing scrutiny. He put his hands to her face, his fingers exploring its contours.

'There's an awful lot of good-looking girls around, but you've got that extra bit of class.'

His hands went down to sweep her body, stroking, poking, prodding. Jo recoiled and he laughed.

'For the moment, this is strictly business.' He nodded. 'You've got a good shape, but women with good bodies are ten a penny.' He gripped her suddenly around the waist, pulling her towards him. 'What a girl needs to get on in this business is a good agent.' His hot breath brushed her cheek. 'You need me, sweetie.' His lips sought her mouth. 'So how about it?'

Jo tried to pull away from him, frightened by the leering face so close to hers. 'I don't want to be a model, Mr Harding,' she said, fear making her breathless. 'All I want is to go home.'

He drew back a little and his narrow eyes looked into hers. 'OK,' he said. 'I'll make sure you get there. Yeah. I'll make sure of that.' He tightened the grip of one hand about her waist and brought the other up to the buttons of her blouse. 'But it's quite a while to noon.' He undid the top button and moved on down to the next. 'So, how about thanking me in advance?'

'Stop it—please.' Jo's voice shook with a mixture of fear and fury, but instinct warned her to stay calm and to use reason. 'I don't want to cause a scene, but if you go any further I'll scream.'

'Go ahead—scream. It happens all the time in places like this. No one will come. No one will risk butting in on something private.'

He was probably speaking the truth, Jo thought bleakly. He had the upper hand and he knew it. He was a small man, but strong, and if he was really determined to rape her Jo knew she would stand little chance against him.

'If you rape me,' she said, as calmly as she could manage, 'I'll call the police.'

'Rape?' He laughed unpleasantly. 'You came here of your own free will. I didn't have to drag you. That guy out there will testify you walked right in here. You weren't making any fuss when he came with the food. Who'd believe it was rape?'

Oh, no! It was all true. Jo felt the panic rising. How could she have been so stupid as not to see this coming? To anyone with an ounce of sense the danger would have been written on the wall a mile high. But her mind hadn't been functioning properly. It had been full of Lee and what had happened between them.

Cy Harding's hand reached suddenly into her hair, dragging her face to his. 'Quit stalling, sweetie. This isn't going to be so bad. You've been there before—

lots of times, I'm sure. Relax. You might even enjoy it. I know I will.'

His mouth closed on hers, cruelly hard, pressing the insides of her lips against her teeth. His hand was groping into her blouse, searching for her breast, and Jo felt the revulsion of his touch.

Desperately, she tried to wrench herself away from him, her scream stifled by the pressure of his mouth. He was dragging her backwards, towards the bed. Jo knew that if he got her there and put his weight on her, she would be lost. Already her strength was beginning to ebb.

The back of her knees was against the bed and he was pressing her forcefully back. Somehow, she managed to bring her knees up as he came down hard on top of her and she heard the breath leave his body as her knees made contact with the lower part of his stomach and his groin.

He yelled with pain and Jo felt his hold slacken. With a tremendous effort, she pushed him back and away from her. He lurched backwards, holding on to himself, his face contorted with pain, and she got up and made for the door. She was tugging at the lock as his hands clutched at her, pulling her around. His hand was raised and, as she stared into his furious face, she wondered if he was going to kill her.

She opened her mouth and screamed.

'Hey! You in there! Is your name Harding?'

The voice from outside seemed almost to speak in Jo's ear as she cowered against the door. Cy Harding's hand, which had been descending, was stayed, and he stared at the door as though it were the wood which had spoken to him.

'What d'ya want?' he gritted harshly.

'There's two guys out here. . .want to speak to you.'

Harding's face was a picture of disbelief.

Jo took advantage of the moment to shove him away from her. She screamed again and grabbed frantically at the lock. 'Oh, please!' she cried. 'Let me out of here!'

She heard the scrape of a key and the door was suddenly opened. Standing on the other side, behind the janitor, was a steely faced Lee and a grinning Mo.

'Let me handle him, Lee,' Mo said. 'It'll be my pleasure.'

'But how did you know where to find me?'

Jo was sitting in the back seat of Lee's large limousine. Lee's arms were wrapped tightly around her and she felt as though she'd jumped straight from hell into heaven.

'The harbour master saw you leaving with your baggage in Cy Harding's car. It wasn't too difficult to work out he'd offered to take you to the airport.'

Jo shook her head, still unable to believe her lucky escape. 'But that place was so out of the way. I couldn't imagine anyone finding it.'

Lee laughed. 'It's only minutes off the highway. It's the nearest motel to the airport—it's used a lot by folk with early or late flights. It was the obvious choice if Harding was planning seduction. Knowing

Harding, it was almost a certainty.' His grip tightened around Jo. 'If we'd been any later. . .' His face
hardened, his eyes glittered like chips of ice. 'He'd
have been taking a trip to the morgue, instead of the
hospital.'

Jo put her hand over his lips. 'Oh, please. I don't
want to think about what might have happened.'

He kissed her fingers and took her hand in his.
'Nor do I.'

He looked pale in the dim light and there was a
dressing taped to the back of his head.

'Should you be out of bed dashing about like this?'
Jo asked axiously. 'What did the doctor say?'

'Later,' he said firmly.

He tucked her head into the hollow of his shoulder
in the now familiar gesture, which brought a strange
and wonderful sensation to Jo's insides.

'Take a nap for now. We'll talk later.' He tilted
her chin and kissed her lips briefly. 'And I warn you,
young lady, I have a great deal to say to you.'

Lee was standing with his back to the fire, the stone
mantel-shelf behind him, and Jo was ensconced on
the settee with a blanket around her and a steaming
cup of tea in her hand.

'It's you who should be wrapped up and cosseted
like this,' she protested. 'The shock has probably
still to come out from that awful fall.' She put down
her cup and held out her hand to him. 'I can't tell
you how sorry I am, Lee. I don't know what I'd have
done if. . .you. . .' Her eyes began to fill up and it

was obvious that her emotions were still running very near to the surface.

He came and took her hand. 'Stop it, Jo,' he said. 'I may spend most of my time behind a desk, but I'm still as tough as any old salt.'

'It was—terrible. . . I thought I'd. . .killed you.' She lowered her head. 'You can't possibly know. . .how I felt.'

Lee snorted. 'I can hazard a guess. I was going through pretty much the same thing when I saw you running into the surf.'

He shook his head. 'What I want to know is why the hell you were doing that. . .rushing out of the house like a mad thing.'

Jo bit her lip. 'I'm sorry. I didn't know myself where I was going or what I intended to do. After I saw Jocelyn's letter, I thought she was coming here. . .and. . .all I could think of was to get away. . .'

'But if you'd read the letter you would have known that Jocelyn is married to Burt Keegan. She wrote to ask if I'd get together with them for a talk—just to make sure there'd be no bad feeling between us when he resumed his seat on the board of directors of my company. Why didn't you read it?'

'It was a private letter,' she protested fiercely. 'I couldn't read it.'

'That damned integrity of yours.' He shook his head at her. 'I guess it's one of the things I like about you, but it can be damned inconvenient at times.'

'It wouldn't have mattered anyway,' Jo said stubbornly. 'I still wouldn't have known how you felt about Jocelyn—if she'd have come here. . .'

'How could you not have known?' he asked a little exasperatedly. 'I'd have thought—after last night—the way we were with one another. . .you should have known it wouldn't have made any difference to you and me if she did come.'

Jo's heart began to pound. 'How could I know that?' she asked in a small voice. 'I thought you were still in love with Jocelyn. That what we. . .did. . .last night was just—one of those things.'

He gave a short, disbelieving laugh. 'Well. If that was just "one of those things" I hope we have lots more of them.'

Her eyes were on his and she dared suddenly to hope. 'Lee—are you still in love with Jocelyn? Was any of it because I reminded you of her?'

He nodded slowly. 'Yes.'

Jo swallowed back the lump which rose in her throat.

'The first five minutes,' Lee went on. 'When I saw you in the hall. I thought you were Jocelyn then.' He grasped her arms and shook her gently. 'But from the first time I held you in my arms. . .the first time I kissed you. . . I knew the difference—and from then on I wanted only you.'

'No,' Jo said disbelievingly. 'I saw it in your face— the hurt—every time I mentioned Jocelyn.'

'Hurt!' Lee echoed. 'Sure. I was hurt. Right here.' He tapped his head. 'In my pride. But not here.' He put her hand to his chest and she could feel the strong, heady rhythm beating there. 'Not in my heart.' He smiled wryly. 'That was where you came in. Kicking me back every time I tried to. . .give you a little—get close to you.'

Jo bit her lip. 'What did you expect, when you told me right from the start that you believed I was only here to get what I could from you?'

He nodded. 'I guess I was a fool in the beginning, but it didn't take me long to realise the kind of a girl you were and then I just couldn't keep from wanting to hold you.'

'Well, you had a damned funny way of showing it,' she said and then sighed, turning her cheek against his throat. 'I wish I'd known—I thought it was because I looked like Jocelyn that you wanted to make love to me.'

He made a soft tutting sound and tightened his hold on her. 'And that was why you had all your lovely hair cut off.' He stroked her head. 'You really didn't have to do that. It's what goes on inside that makes you the girl I love.'

Jo gasped and sat up, her eyes wide. 'That's the first time. . .you've. . .mentioned. . .love.'

He stared back at her, a teasing light in his eyes. 'It is?' He kissed her on the tip of her nose. 'I'll remember to mention it more often in the future. But I'd have thought it was all too obvious.

'Not to me it wasn't.' She gave a shaky laugh. 'And then—there was Stacey.'

'Yeah! Stacey!' He smiled sardonically. 'I guess you didn't have much faith in my morals. You

believed I was sleeping with Stacey and all the while
trying to make love to you?'

'She waited for you to come back—that first night.
And then almost every night afterwards her bunk
was empty.

He nodded. 'She waited, sure. But it was to make
certain I was safely in my cabin before going to Mo.
It was always Mo she wanted.'

'No.' Jo shook her head. 'It was always you she
danced with—you she kept shining up to.'

'Yeah. But it was Mo she was trying to bring up
to scratch. She hated the way you two seemed always
to be together.' He grinned wryly. 'I guess I did
too.'

'You were jealous,' she teased.

He nodded sheepishly. 'I thought I had reason to
be.'

'It was only friendship,' Jo defended. 'You were
so cool—so distant. I had to have someone to talk
to.'

'It didn't look that way. And I guess that's why
Stacey had to try so hard to get his attention.' He
laughed. 'Well! She finally made it and led him right
up to the altar.'

Jo nodded soberly. 'Yes. I do hope she will make
him happy.'

'That's not your concern. Mo can take care of
himself.' He tilted her face up to his. 'Right now, I
could do with a little attention myself.'

He kissed her mouth sweetly, persuasively.

'How about you making *me* happy. . .by saying
you'll marry me?'

Jo caught her breath. 'Oh! Lee! Do you really mean it? But——'

He stopped her with another kiss, deeper and infinitely more satisfying, and her senses were spinning dizzily when he finally lifted his head.

'All I want to hear from you now is one word,' he said firmly.

Jo said it. 'Yes.'

Next month's Romances

Each month, you can choose from a world of variety in romance with Mills & Boon. These are the new titles to look out for next month.

A PROMISE TO REPAY Amanda Browning
SHOTGUN WEDDING Charlotte Lamb
SUCH SWEET POISON Anne Mather
PERILOUS REFUGE Patricia Wilson
PASSIONATE BETRAYAL Jacqueline Baird
AN UNEQUAL PARTNERSHIP Rosemary Gibson
HAPPY ENDING Sandra Field
KISS AND SAY GOODBYE Stephanie Howard
SCANDALOUS SEDUCTION Miranda Lee
BACKLASH Elizabeth Oldfield
ANGELA'S AFFAIR Vanessa Grant
WINDSWEPT Rosalie Henaghan
TIGER MOON Kristy McCallum
THE PRICE OF DESIRE Kate Proctor
COUNTRY BRIDE Debbie Macomber

STARSIGN
DARK PASSION Sally Heywood

Available from Boots, Martins, John Menzies, W.H. Smith, Woolworths and other paperback stockists.

Also available from Mills and Boon Reader Service, P.O. Box 236, Thornton Road, Croydon, Surrey CR9 3RU.

Life and death drama
in this gripping new novel
of passion and suspense

Following a vicious attack on a tough property developer and his beautiful wife, eminent surgeon David Compton fought fiercely to save both lives, little knowing just how deeply he would become involved in a complex web of deadly revenge. Ginette Irving, the cool and practical theatre sister, was an enigma to David, but could he risk an affair with the worrying threat to his career and now the sinister attempts on his life?

W●RLDWIDE

Price: £3.99   Published: May 1991

Available from Boots, Martins, John Menzies, W.H. Smith,
Woolworths and other paperback stockists.
Also available from Mills and Boon Reader Service, P.O. Box 236,
Thornton Road, Croydon, Surrey CR9 3RU

Relax in the sun with our Summer Reading Selection

Four new Romances by favourite authors, Anne Beaumont, Sandra Marton, Susan Napier and Yvonne Whittal, have been specially chosen by Mills & Boon to help you escape from it all this Summer.

Price: £5.80. Published: July 1991

Available from Boots, Martins, John Menzies, W.H. Smith, Woolworths and other paperback stockists.

Also available from Mills and Boon Reader Service, P.O. Box 236, Thornton Road, Croydon, Surrey CR9 3RU.